STORIES FOR LITTLE ONES

Illustrated by
CATHIE SHUTTLEWORTH

Written by
NICOLA BAXTER

ARMADILLO

This edition published in 2002 by
Armadillo Books
An imprint of Bookmart Limited
Desford Road, Enderby
Leicester, LE19 4AD

© 1999 Bookmart Limited

Originally produced by Bookmart as
The Teddy Bear Collection,
The Bunny Tales Collection and
The Puppy Tales Collection.

Produced by: Nicola Baxter
Editorial Consultant: Ronnie Randall
Designer: Amanda Hawkes

ISBN 1-84322-134-9

Printed in Italy

STORIES
FOR
LITTLE ONES

*I'd like my wedding dress to have spider lace
and rose-petal ribbons*

RIBBONS AND LACE, page 163.

THE
TEDDY BEAR
COLLECTION

On cold winter nights, there is nothing bears like better than cuddling up together in front of a glowing fire and telling each other teddy bear tales. Most of all, they like to tell stories about themselves—real bear stories about their lives when non-bears are not there.

Now, for the first time, the Growling (the Chief Council of Bear Affairs) has agreed that some of these stories can be told.

What really happened on the Teddy Bears' Picnic? Where do all the little lost bears go? What happens if a teddy bear meets a *real* bear? Are there bears so tiny you can't see them at all?

Read this collection of exciting, scary, funny, silly stories to learn more about bears than most non-bears ever discover.

Pictures tell stories too from age to age;
Search here and there
For the pawprint of a bear
Hidden on every page.

CONTENTS

THE
BUNNY TALES
COLLECTION

Y ou don't often see a bunny by herself. That is because
bunnies like nothing better than being together, snuggling
up in their warm burrows as one big, happy family. Of course,
those burrows can be pretty noisy places, with everyone trying
to talk at once.

Bunnies love to tell stories, and you can read some of them
in this book. They are all about the bunnies who live in Warren
Wood, far away beneath the great oak tree.

Do you know what happens when a bunny eats too much
fudge? Or gets too friendly with a fox? Or tries to make a
wedding dress at the very last minute?

Read this collection of bunny stories and you will soon find
out. If you look very carefully at the pictures, you will find lots
of hidden surprises there, too.

Pictures tell stories too from age to age;
If you search you may spot
One carrot (or a lot!)
Hidden on every page.

CONTENTS

THE
PUPPY TALES
COLLECTION

I don't know if you have every visited the fine town of Houndsville. No? Well, it is home to the finest pack of dogs you could ever hope to meet—and the naughtiest puppies, too! You can meet Houndsville's most famous citizens in the stories in this book. Look out for Mr. Bones the Baker, Duchess Dulay, Dasher the Delivery Dog, and many others.

There is always something going on in Houndsville. What happened to Duchess Dulay's diamond bracelet? Was Mr. Terrier the Teacher really attacked by an alien life form? Why is Mrs. Gruff the Greengrocer so tired these days? Why was Sir Woofington Paws so pleased to meet a thief in his house?

You will soon know the answers to all these questions, and if you look very carefully at the pictures, you will find lots of hidden surprises there, as well.

Pictures tell stories too from age to age;
If you search you may spot
One bone (or a lot!)
Hidden on every page.

CONTENTS

Next morning, the whole village gathered in amazement
at the foot of the hill. Overnight, the castle had changed
in an extraordinary way.

THE GHOSTLY BEAR, page 55

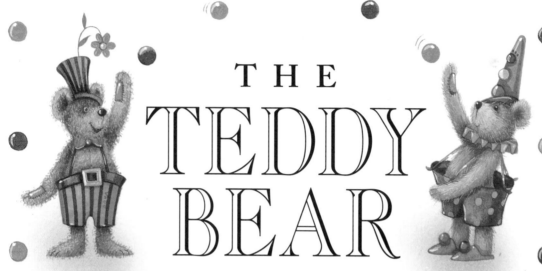

THE
TEDDY
BEAR
COLLECTION

Illustrated by
CATHIE SHUTTLEWORTH

Written by
NICOLA BAXTER

The Real Story of

THE TEDDY BEARS' PICNIC

Colonel Augustus Bearington (retired) here! Young bears, a lot of stuff and nonsense has been said about the illustrious event known as the Teddy Bears' Picnic. Of course, very few of the fine bears who were present that day still have all their stitching. I was only a young bear myself, but I remember it so well. The time has come to set the record straight. Throw another log on the fire, Mungo. My threadbare old ears feel the cold.

First of all, you must remember that things were different in those days. Today you young bears live in households that may have four or five bears. You have company and can rely on each other in times of trouble. In my young days, bears were less common. Only very lucky children lived with a bear of their own. A bear might stay in the same household for fifty years, passed down from father to son or kept on a shelf in the nursery.

Nurseries! That was another big difference. Children who shared their homes with bears usually spent most of their time in the nursery with a woman called a nanny. She looked after the children while their mother and father were busy, which was all the time except for half an hour in the evening. You may well growl, Mungo. Those nannies did a job that any self-respecting bear could do in his sleep.

Children had to be seen and not heard in those days, and nannies got very cross indeed if they didn't wash behind their ears. Things are very different today. Very different indeed.

In those days, bears were not able to meet very often. The best chance was in the afternoon, when nannies took their charges to the park. Then children would play with friends from other big houses, nannies would chat and knit with other nannies, and bears, of course, could have a word with other bears. It was a part of the day that every bear looked forward to. Luckily, the nanny in the house where I lived liked nothing better than a long chat with her friends. No one paid any attention if a bear strolled off and kept up with his own social life.

I think it was Rufus who first put the idea into our heads. Rufus was a reddish-brown bear from a rather well-to-do home. The little girl he lived with was a Lady. Yes, a real Lady, whose mother was a Duchess. I have moved in very elevated circles in my time, Mungo. I must say that Rufus didn't let his titled family go to his head. He was a friendly, straightforward bear, who never put on airs and graces.

One day, Rufus arrived with interesting news. The Duke and Duchess were giving a party for some Very Important People. There were whispers that the Queen herself would be coming.

"You know, Gussie," said Rufus, "we bears should have a party of our own. We could invite all the Most Important Bears in town and have a day to remember."

Well, the idea caught on at once. Every bear for miles around got wind of the plan somehow, and we soon had a guest list of over a hundred.

"The problem, Rufus old chap," I said one day, "is to find a place big enough for a party of this size. We can't run the risk of being discovered, you know."

Rufus didn't hesitate for a moment.

"We'll hold it right here," he said.

It was obvious! I was a muttonhead not to have thought of it myself. After that, there was no time to lose. I was in charge of arrangements, of course. It takes a military mind to organize an event on that scale. And, modesty aside, I must confess that I also came up with the date for the picnic. Army training came in useful for that, too.

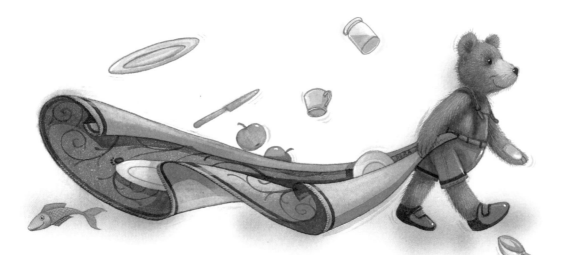

Luckily, several young bears helped with the preparations. You'd be amazed what can be smuggled among a baby's blankets. There were cups, saucers, plates, and food, of course. And some cushions for the old bears. Damp grass is not good for their fur, you know.

At last the great day arrived. It was the day of the Queen's Jubilee. She had been on the throne for umpteen years, and her subjects lined the streets to cheer. Meanwhile, dozens of little bears padded along the back streets, heading for the picnic of a lifetime.

What an afternoon that was! I've never seen so many bears having so much fun.

Ah, and that was the afternoon I met Rosabella. But that's another story.

What was that you said, Mungo? Yes, someone did see us. I don't know who it was. Yes, there was a song. It was quite popular, although the facts were wrong, of course. We were nowhere near the woods. All make believe? Just you look here, young bears. I've carried this worn photograph in my breast pocket for over sixty years.

Ah, yes. It brings a lump to my throat just to look at all those fine faces. Bears were bears in those days. Stir that fire up, Mungo. The smoke's getting in my eyes. Whose turn is it next for a story?

The Amazing Story of
THE BEAR WITH BELLS

Thank you, Colonel. I'm new to your circle, so
let me introduce myself. I'm Hermann P. Bear
from Switzerland. No, I don't know what the P.
stands for, I'm afraid. Now, with all respect, I've
found that today's bears are just as brave and
clever as the noble bears of yesterday. My story
proves just that. And it didn't happen so very long
ago, either.

The story concerns a friend of mine, back home among the mountains. I'll call him Fritz. That is not his real name, but he is a modest bear and, if he ever appears in public again, he would not want the world to know the part he played in the Great Zurich Bank Robbery.

Now Fritz is the cleverest, kindest, jolliest bear you could ever hope to meet, but since the day he was sewn, he has suffered a great hardship. Around his neck, his toymaker has put a collar of jingling, jangling, clinking, clanking, ting-a-linging tiny bells.

I can see how horrified you are to hear this. Yes, poor Fritz could not creep off to see his friends during the night. He could not stretch his legs during the day, in case his owner heard him. He was forced to sit quite still, hour after hour, for fear of revealing the great secret of bearness.

Now Fritz was such an unusual bear that he
was bought by a collector. Yes, a grown-up person
who had over a hundred very beautiful bears. I
myself ... *ahem* ... was one of them. The grown-up
was a very rich gentleman, who, in all honesty,
cared more about money than bears. He loved us
for the francs (that's Swiss money) we were worth,
not for the very fine bears we all were.

One day, this gentleman went to America to buy some more bears. While he was gone, he put all his dearest possessions in the bank, and that included some of us bears. It was dreadful. We were kept in a trunk in a large safe-deposit box, where a bear had only to move a whisker to set off dozens of alarms and sirens. I soon learned to admire Fritz even more. Imagine living like that all the time!

We had been in the bank for two long weeks, when the Great Robbery took place. Of course, we knew very little about it, inside our trunk. We heard the explosion and felt ourselves being jiggled about as the trunk was carried out, but we only guessed what had happened, as we could see very little through the keyhole of the trunk.

It was some hours later, in a cold Swiss dawn, that the robbers arrived at their hideaway—a cave tucked away in the side of a mountain. They hid their truck among some trees nearby and set about dividing up their ill-gotten gains.

All went well as they opened the boxes containing jewels and gold coins. Then the lid of our trunk was roughly opened and a very unpleasant man peered inside.

I'm afraid that his language, when he saw us sitting there, was quite unrepeatable, especially in front of you younger bears. My ears turned quite pink, I can tell you.

The stupid man had no idea we were valuable
bears at all. He kicked the trunk so hard it toppled
over, and we fell onto the cold floor of the cave,
with icicles dripping down on us. My fur has never
been the same since.

It was almost dark when we heard noises
outside. It was the police! They had followed the
tracks of the robbers' truck to the nearby trees.
Now the cave was very well hidden. All the
robbers had to do was keep still.

"There was probably a helicopter waiting," I heard a policeman say. "They won't be here now." Now, as you know, humans cannot hear bear speech, so we were powerless to make a noise, but Fritz was a very brave bear indeed. He jumped to his feet and began to jingle and jangle as hard as he could. Every bell around his neck was clinking and clanking. In the silence, it seemed to be an enormous noise.

The most vicious-looking of the robbers—and none of them resembled angels—leaped toward Fritz with a murderous cry. At that moment, a powerful flashlight lit the dramatic scene.

Well, the rest is history. The robbers were
caught, the loot was recovered, and we bears were
taken into custody as evidence. None of the
humans realized whom they had to thank, of
course. But then, we all know that they do not
have our education. Eventually, we were sold to
new owners, all over the world.

And Fritz? Well, I cannot be quite sure. He fell
behind a boulder and was not discovered with the
rest of us. There are sometimes stories of a strange
tinkling, jingling sound to be heard in the
mountains, as though a bear with bells around his
neck might be skidding happily down the slopes.
One or two people have found strange pawprints
in the snow. I hope that Fritz is happy, living the
life of a free and furry bear.

But if you should ever find yourselves in danger in the Alps, dear friends, you might call out the name of Hermann P. Bear. I like to think that a very old friend of mine would come to your aid.

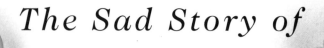

The Sad Story of

THE LITTLE LOST BEARS

The story of Fritz, my friends, has made me think of a subject that is important to all of us. I am speaking, of course, of lost bears. All of us, perhaps, have known bears who have been lost by careless humans. When I was very small, my mother said to me, "Belinda Bear, always stay close to your owner, especially on trains, for there are many little bears today sitting in Lost Property Offices, never to find their way home." I have never forgotten her words.

Well, when I was a little bear, I did not always listen to my mother as well as I should. My friend Bessie and I got into all kinds of trouble. We spent more time in the bathtub than any bear would wish, having jelly, or paint, or honey washed out of our fur. But although we were often in disgrace, we were always careful not to get lost. The idea of the Lost Property Office was *too* horrible. We made sure that the little girl who looked after us *never* left us behind.

One day, Maisie (that was the little girl's name) went to visit her grandmother. And she went by train! Bessie and I were very worried.

"Let's hold paws all the time," said Bessie. "Then, if we get lost, at least we will be together."

So Bessie and I went with Maisie on the train. And I can tell you that trains are *not* safe places for bears. First a large lady put her shopping bag down on top of us and squashed one of my ears. Luckily, Maisie noticed and asked her to move it.

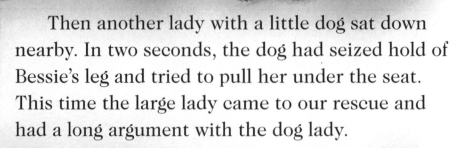

Then another lady with a little dog sat down nearby. In two seconds, the dog had seized hold of Bessie's leg and tried to pull her under the seat. This time the large lady came to our rescue and had a long argument with the dog lady.

Of course, we expect humans to be silly. They don't have a bear's sharp brain, after all. But it was the train itself that caused our biggest problem. With every jiggle and jounce, it jolted us nearer and nearer to the edge of the seat. And let me tell you, those trains jiggle and jounce all the time!

It was sure to happen. As the train rumbled around a corner, we tumbled onto the floor and rolled under the table. At that moment, every single non-bear in the compartment was asleep, including Maisie and the annoying little dog.

"We'll be left on the train," I moaned. "Then it will be the Lost Property Office for us."

But Bessie had one of her Good Ideas. Bessie's Good Ideas are sometimes very, very good and sometimes very, very bad. I listened carefully.

"If we climb inside Maisie's overnight bag," she said, "we can't be left behind."

I thought about it. It *did* seem to be a good idea. We climbed into the bag and fell fast asleep. That jiggling, jouncing train has a lot to answer for.

It was dark when we woke up, and we could tell we were no longer on the train.

"We must be in Maisie's grandmother's house," Bessie whispered. Maisie will come soon."

Sure enough, we soon heard footsteps. The bag was opened and a face looked down at us. It was the large lady from the train!

I don't know which of us was more surprised. "Look!" she called to her husband. "These bears belonged to the little girl on the train. What can I do with them?"

It was then that we heard the words we had been dreading.

"Take them to the Lost Property Office," said the man.

"Whatever happens," whispered Bessie, "we mustn't end up you-know-where. We'll escape."

"Is that one of your Good Ideas?" I asked suspiciously.

"No," said Bessie, "it's the only idea there is."

So late that night, when the moon was high in the sky, we crawled out of a downstairs window and set off for home, not knowing which direction to follow or how far away we were.

When morning came, we found we were deep in a forest. Paw in paw, we wandered through the trees, looking for signs that humans were near.

Day after day, we walked on sore paws. We ate berries from the bushes and slept on the soft moss among the roots of the trees. Once a bad bird tried to peck out our fur to line its nest, but Bessie was good at growling and frightened it away. Once I fell into a hole in a tree and only just managed to climb out again.

At night, we often cried ourselves to sleep.

One afternoon, we were found by a family taking a walk. The little girl brought me here to join you all and gave Bessie to her cousin. From that day to this, I have never seen Bessie or Maisie, and my furry face is often wet with tears. If there were human children listening to me now, I would tell them to cuddle their bears and keep them safe, for in my dreams, I often see Maisie's little face and hope that she has found a new bear to make her happy.

The Scary Story of

THE GHOSTLY BEAR

Little bears, the story I am about to tell is very, very scary. If you get frightened, you must put your paws over your ears and cuddle up to a grown-up bear.

When I was a very little bear myself, my aunty told me this tale. She was a very sensible bear, so I am sure that every word is true.

Once upon a time, in a faraway land, there was a huge castle. It was tall and dark. Vines covered the turrets and many of the dusty windows. Bats fluttered from the battlements.

The castle stood empty for many years, but one day there was great excitement in the nearby village. It was said that the owner of the castle was coming to visit. Now no one had ever seen this mysterious owner, so there was a great deal of talk about who it might be.

"I've heard it is a Countess," said the baker. "She was once very beautiful. Then a witch put a curse on her. Since then she has always worn a veil to hide her ugly face."

"No, no," replied the blacksmith, "the owner *is* a witch. She travels at night, and has a black cat."

"Nonsense!" The schoolteacher waved her stick. "It is simply an old lady who cannot move around very well. That is why she has not visited for a long time."

Every day, the children in the village looked out for the important visitor, but no one came along the winding road from the forest. Then, one morning, a little girl called Lucy noticed smoke rising above the highest tower in the castle.

"She must have come in the night!" she called to everyone she met. "She is a witch after all."

When they heard this, the villagers were very worried. "We must take her a big present," they said, "so she does not get angry with us. Who knows what spells she might cast if she feels we are unfriendly."

That seemed to be a good idea, so a collection was made and a beautiful chest was bought to be given to the witch (if that was what she was).

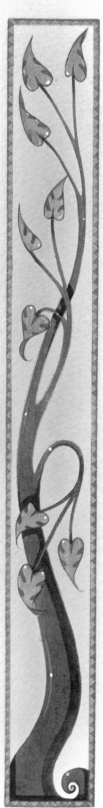

"Now," said the baker, "who will give the present to the witch? I cannot go with my weak heart and that long, winding path to climb."

"Nor can I," said the teacher, "with my bad leg."

For one reason or another, not one of the grown-ups in the village could deliver the present to the mysterious visitor.

"I'll go," said Lucy. "I'd like to see what she looks like."

"But," said the blacksmith, "won't you be frightened?"

"Oh no," replied Lucy. "I will take my teddy bear with me. He'll keep me safe."

She certainly was a very sensible little girl.

That afternoon, Lucy set off to the castle, carrying her bear and the chest. It was a long climb up the winding path, but at last she stood before the doors of the castle and knocked.

As she stood there, all by herself, Lucy began to feel just a little bit frightened. But she clutched her old bear and started to sing to keep her spirits up. For a long time, nothing happened. Then, with a horrible creaking noise, the doors of the castle slowly opened—all by themselves.

There really was not much to do but walk straight in, and Lucy was beginning to feel that anything was better than standing on the doorstep.

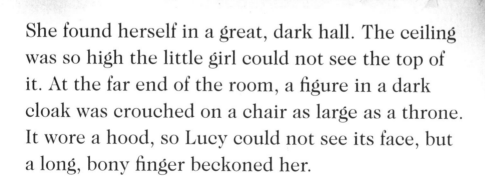

She found herself in a great, dark hall. The ceiling was so high the little girl could not see the top of it. At the far end of the room, a figure in a dark cloak was crouched on a chair as large as a throne. It wore a hood, so Lucy could not see its face, but a long, bony finger beckoned her.

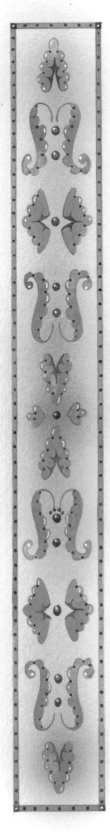

When the little girl was standing in front of the figure at last, she tried to speak up bravely, though there was a quiver in her voice.

"Please, your highness, or your witchness, we all wanted to welcome you to the castle and give you this present."

A horrible cackle came from the dark-robed figure. "A chest? I've got hundreds of them," it croaked. "But I can see that you do have something I want. Give me that teddy bear, and I will let you go home safely."

"No!" cried Lucy, hugging her teddy bear. "You can't have him."

"Really?" replied the voice. "Then I shall have to lock you up until you agree."

The next thing Lucy knew, she was being dragged into a room containing an enormous four-poster bed, and the door of the room was being locked behind her.

Lucy stayed in that room until it began to get dark. Then the dark figure brought her some food and a single candle.

"Go to bed," it said. "Let's see if you feel so brave in the morning."

Lucy climbed into bed and pulled the covers
up to her chin. She felt more frightened than she
ever had in her life, but somehow, she managed to
go to sleep.

At midnight, she was woken by a clock clanging loudly near her bed.

Dong! Dong! Dong!

She woke to find a large, white bear standing by her bed. He seemed to be shimmering with a strange light.

"W...w...what do you want?" she asked.

The strange bear said nothing, but it held out its furry paws toward Lucy's little bear, tucked up beside her in the bed.

"No!" cried Lucy. "He's mine!"

But then she saw an extraordinary thing. Large crystal tears were running down the shining bear's face and dripping onto the little girl's bed.

He looked so very sad that Lucy could not bear
it. "All right," she said quietly. "Don't be sad.
Here's my own special bear to cheer you up." And
she handed her own teddy bear to the strange,
ghostly visitor.

With a sigh, holding the
little bear gently in his arms,
the shining bear turned
away. Lucy watched as he
walked toward the door
… and melted straight
through it! Lucy shut her
eyes and rubbed them. When
she opened them, she was back
in her own room at home, tucked up in her own
little bed. Only her teddy bear was missing.

Next morning, the whole village gathered in amazement at the foot of the hill. Overnight, the castle had changed in an extraordinary way. The windows were sparkling. The vine had been cut. There were flags flying from the turrets and white doves fluttering around the battlements.

"It must have been bewitched after all," gasped the villagers. "Our act of kindness in sending the chest has broken the spell. That is often the way in old stories."

Lucy thought about what had happened. She thought about the chest hidden under her bed.

"Someone was unhappy," she thought. "And now they are not. That is what bears are for."

I believe she was right, my friends. The mystery never was solved. Later it was said that the Countess who lived in the castle had suffered an unhappy childhood. Perhaps returning to the castle of her birth had brought a smile to her face again. Only Lucy had a different idea.

The Funny Story of

THE BEAR WHO WAS BARE

My dears, after that rather scary tale, I have one that is not in the least bit frightening. You can come out from behind that chair, young bears. Uncle Bill Bear has a much sillier tale to tell you. This story is about a bare bear. A bare bear? I mean, of course, a bear wearing nothing at all— not even his fur! Let me tell you how it happened.

Once there was a bear called Edwin Dalrymple Devereux Yeldon III. He said that his friends called him Eddy, but as a matter of fact, this bear did not have many friends at all. And that was because he was simply not a very nice bear. Oh, he was very handsome, with long, golden fur that shone in the sunlight, but that was where the problem began. Eddy thought he was better than other bears, with his long name and fancy fur.

"Pass me my fur brush," he would say. "The breeze has ruffled me terribly. You other bears need not worry, of course, with your short, rough, ordinary fur."

When the bears played leap-bear or hide-and-seek in the nursery, Eddy always refused to play. "Those are very rough games," he complained. "I might get my paws dirty. Games are too silly for superior bears like myself."

Well, after a while, all the other bears were sick of Edwin and his airs and graces. I'm afraid that some young bears tried to think of ways of teaching Eddy a lesson. But as things turned out, they did not need to. Edwin Dalrymple Devereux Yeldon III brought about his own downfall.

One day, Eddy was boasting about all the famous bears he knew. One or two of the other bears wondered out loud if his tales were really true, which made Eddy furious. "You'll see," he said. "I'll write a letter to my friend Prince Bearovski. He's sure to write back at once, and then you'll see."

But as Eddy carried a huge bottle of ink across the room, his furry feet tripped on the edge of the rug. Down fell teddy Eddy. Up flew the bottle of ink. *Splat!* The bottle hit the floor, and ink flew everywhere! There was ink on Eddy's nose and ink on his ears. His paws and his knees had bright blue splashes too. For a second, there was silence. Then Eddy let out a horrible roar. "You stupid bears!" he cried. "Just look at my fur! Who put that rug in the way?" And that was really not very fair, for the rug had been there for years and years.

Teddy Eddy sulked for the rest of the day. But worse was to follow. Next morning, the little girl who lived there saw what had happened to her most beautiful bear. Without asking anyone else at all, she decided that Eddy needed a bath.

The other bears peeked around the bathroom door to watch the proceedings. There were bubbles everywhere! Only the tip of teddy Eddy's nose could be seen. Giggling and chuckling, the bears went back to the nursery and waited for Eddy to reappear.

They waited all that day and all that night. But Eddy did not return. Next day, there was no sign of him.

"That little girl is not very sensible," said one bear. "She may have left him in the water. We really should go and see if he's all right, my friends."

But teddy Eddy was not in the bathtub. The bears were just about to go away again, when one little bear noticed that one of the cupboards was not quite closed.

Inside sat Edwin Dalrymple Devereux Yeldon III, wrapped from ears to paws in a large towel.

"Come on, Eddy," called the young bear mischievously, "you must be dry by now."

"No," said Eddy. "I … er … I can't."

"But it must be very boring in this cupboard," said another bear.

"No," said Eddy. "It's … er … very pleasant. Please go away."

"Oh come on," laughed two of the smallest bears. And they tugged playfully at the towel. Eddy tried hard to hold onto it, but it was no use. As the towel slipped away, every bear could see … Edwin Dalrymple Devereux Yeldon III was bare! When the little girl washed away the ink, Eddy's fur was washed away too.

Poor Eddy. He couldn't hide any more. Slowly, he walked back to the nursery and sat down in the darkest corner. The old, proud Edwin Dalrymple Devereux Yeldon III was gone. A very different bear remained.

For a few days, the other bears smiled to
themselves about what had happened. But after a
while, they began to feel rather sorry for Eddy.

"I think we should help him," said one old
bear. "Apart from anything else, he must be rather
cold without his fur."

"That's true," said another bear. "Why don't
we make him some clothes?"

Over the next few days, the bears had great
fun. They used up all the old scraps of material
that they could find and made some very grand
clothes. There was a hat with a feather, a cloak
with tassels, some striped trousers, and some
shiny black boots.

When he saw them, Eddy was overwhelmed by the bears' kindness.

"Thank you, my friends," he said, as he put on the clothes. "I know that I have not been a very nice bear in the past, but I will try to do better now. In following all that is good and kind and bearlike, I will be absolutely fearless. Or perhaps I should say, in spite of my fine clothes, my dears, absolutely furless!"

The Short Story of

THE LITTLEST BEAR

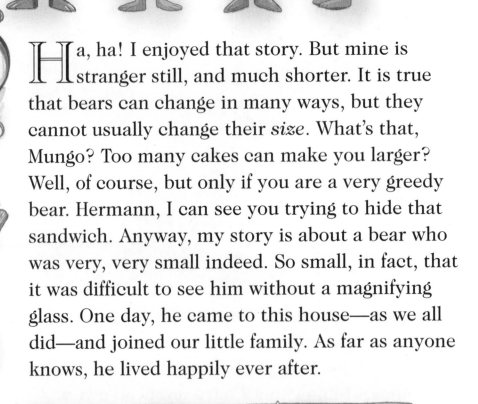

Ha, ha! I enjoyed that story. But mine is stranger still, and much shorter. It is true that bears can change in many ways, but they cannot usually change their *size*. What's that, Mungo? Too many cakes can make you larger? Well, of course, but only if you are a very greedy bear. Hermann, I can see you trying to hide that sandwich. Anyway, my story is about a bear who was very, very small indeed. So small, in fact, that it was difficult to see him without a magnifying glass. One day, he came to this house—as we all did—and joined our little family. As far as anyone knows, he lived happily ever after.

What? No, there isn't any more to the story.
I told you it was short. The bear was so small that
he disappeared on the day he came here and has
never been seen since. I imagine he is here with
us now, but it would take a bear with sharper eyes
than mine to see him. Why don't you all take a
look around?

The Unusual Story of
THE REAL TEDDY BEAR

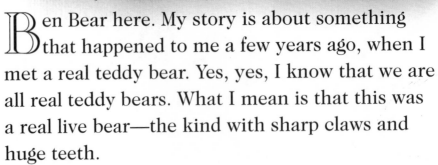

Ben Bear here. My story is about something that happened to me a few years ago, when I met a real teddy bear. Yes, yes, I know that we are all real teddy bears. What I mean is that this was a real live bear—the kind with sharp claws and huge teeth.

Here is what happened. My owner at the time was a little boy who was very fond of food. Wherever we went, he always made sure that he had a bag of goodies with him. "Just in case," he said, "we get caught in an avalanche, or stranded in the desert, or trapped by a flood." Not one of those things was at all likely to happen, but Joseph (that was his name) felt happier if he had some provisions with him.

You can imagine that this was particularly true when he went camping with his friends. All the boys brought food to cook on the campfire, but Joseph brought extra supplies, just in case.

One year, we went deep into the woods. The boys put up their tents and went off to explore. Joseph left me in his tent. Now that I am an older and wiser bear, I realize that he did not want his friends to see me, in case they thought he was a baby. But Joseph looked at me very seriously and said, "Now Ben, your job is to stay here and guard the food!" And I was a young bear who took his job seriously in those days.

The boys were gone for a long time. At first I could hear their shouts echoing through the trees, but soon there was silence. Only the wind could be heard, rustling the branches.

I believe I dozed off for a while, because the next thing I knew, I was wide awake and listening to a very different sound. It was a snorting, sniffling, crunching, munching sort of a noise. I wasn't frightened, of course, but I did wish I knew just what was stomping and chomping outside the tent.

The sounds got louder and louder. Then I heard the sound of the tent flap being unzipped. *Zoooooooooooooooop!*

A brown furry face peered in. It was a bear! A real bear!

For a long, long moment, I looked at the bear.
And the bear looked at me. Then, all of a sudden,
he opened his mouth and said, "Hello! Anything
to eat in here?"

Well, you could have knocked me down
with a feather. He was speaking bear
language, of course, but I found it was
not very different from the way we
teddy bears speak, so I could
understand him fairly well. He
seemed friendly, and I was just
thinking how nice it would be
to get to know him, when I
remembered what Joseph
had said to me.

"No," I said firmly.
"No food in here at all."

But the bear was already sniffing the air and looking suspiciously at the large bag beside me.

"Really?" he said. "That's very strange. I'm pretty sure I can smell sausages and beans and chocolate cake."

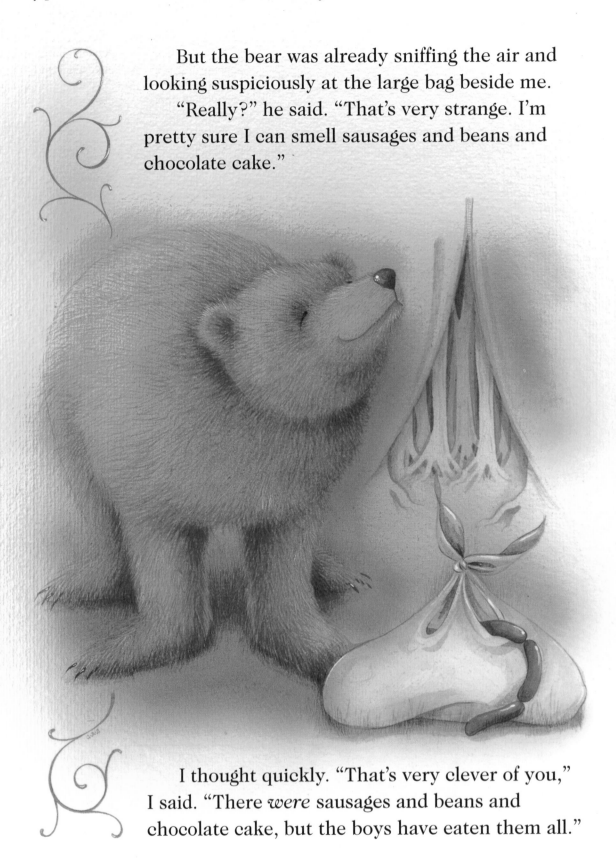

I thought quickly. "That's very clever of you," I said. "There *were* sausages and beans and chocolate cake, but the boys have eaten them all."

"Any leftovers?" asked the bear. "Any crumbs at all?"

"None at all," I replied, shaking my head sadly.

"More supplies coming?" asked the bear eagerly. "Tomorrow, perhaps?"

"I don't think so," I answered. "We're going home in the morning."

The bear nodded his head. "Ho hum," he said. "It's my birthday, you know. I just thought I might find a birthday treat around her somewhere. Well, nice meeting you." And as he ambled away into the forest, I was quite sure I could hear his furry tummy rumbling.

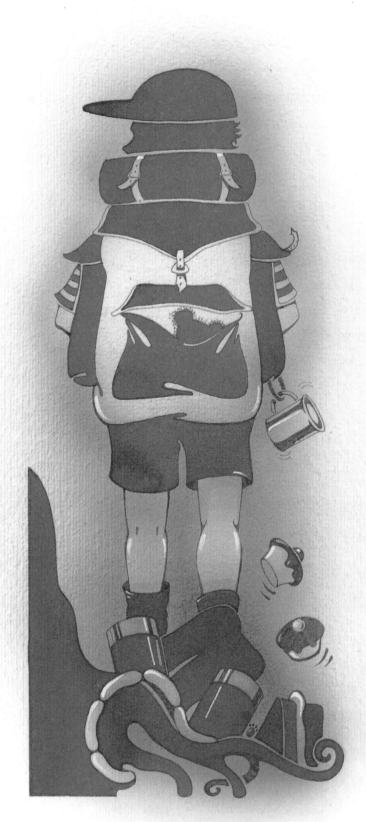

A little while later, the boys came back and made their supper. I kept a wary eye on the shadows between the trees, expecting to see some large furry ears or a sniffly snout. But there was no sign of the bear at all.

Next morning, as planned, we packed up our things and set off for home.

"Now, have we got everything?" asked Joseph. "Let's go!"

By this stage, of course, I was well hidden in Joseph's backpack, so that the other boys would not see me. Otherwise I might have mentioned to him that the special emergency supplies bag had fallen behind the stump of a tree, helped along just a bit by a nudge from my elbow.

Joseph was a little upset when he found that his goodies were gone. But it was far too late to go back into the dark forest to find them, and after all, there were plenty more at home.

As I sat on Joseph's pillow that night, I looked up at the big yellow moon peeking in at the window and imagined the friendly bear, sitting down in the moonlight to enjoy a special snack.

"Happy birthday, bear," I whispered. "Happy birthday!"

The Silly Story of

THE BUZZING BEAR

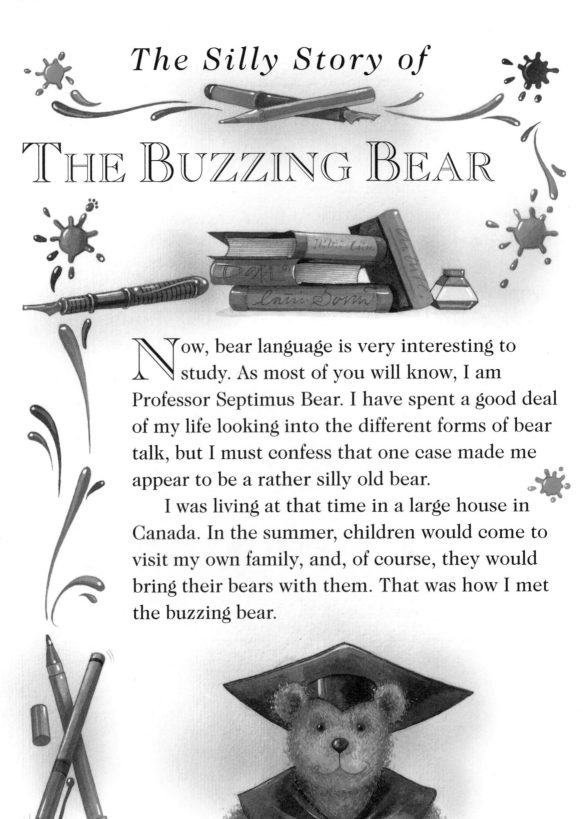

Now, bear language is very interesting to study. As most of you will know, I am Professor Septimus Bear. I have spent a good deal of my life looking into the different forms of bear talk, but I must confess that one case made me appear to be a rather silly old bear.

I was living at that time in a large house in Canada. In the summer, children would come to visit my own family, and, of course, they would bring their bears with them. That was how I met the buzzing bear.

This bear came to the house on a fine, sunny day. He was a large, fluffy bear, with golden yellow fur. Of course, I tried to make him welcome.

"Good morning," I said. "My name is Septimus. Will you tell me yours?"

"Buzz!" said the bear.

"Er … Buzz? Well, it's very nice to meet you, Mr. Buzz. Have you had a long journey?"

"Buzz!" said the bear.

"I'm sorry? Did you say that you have come from far away?"

"Buzz! Buzz! Buzz!" said the strange bear.

Well, I must admit, I was puzzled. I went straight to my reference books to find out if there was a distant country where bears only buzzed. I read and read until darkness fell.

But all my research was in vain. I read about the hooting bears of Borneo and the singing bears of Thailand. I found an article about an African bear language that has all kinds of sounds in it and is impossible for other bears to pronounce. But I could find nothing at all about buzzing bears.

At first I was disappointed. Then I realized the great opportunity that had been presented to me. I could be the very first bear to study this extraordinary language. I saw myself giving lectures to other clever bears around the world. I imagined signing copies of my famous book on the subject. A rosy future was surely before me.

At once, I picked up a new notebook and pencil and set off to find the bear.

The buzzing bear was sitting rather sadly in a chair. I sat down beside him and began to take notes as I asked him questions.

"Are you a bear?" I asked.

"Buzz!" he said.

Aha, I thought, one buzz means yes.

"Are you an elephant?" I asked.

"Buzz! BUZZ!" said the bear.

I decided that two buzzes must mean no.

"Are you a giraffe?" I enquired.

"Buzz!"

My friends, I admit, I was very confused. Then I suddenly realized that the bear might not be able to understand me at all! But how was I to learn buzz language in order to speak to him? I did not know how to say the simplest thing.

It was a beautiful day, so I took the bear by the arm and led him gently out into the garden. By the house was an enormous cedar tree. I led the bear up to it and patted its trunk firmly.

"Tree," I said. "Tree."

"Buzz!" said the bear.

I walked over to a shady seat.

"Chair," I repeated, pointing. "Chair. Chair."

You can probably guess what the bear said.

After half an hour, I was at my wit's end. We had made no progress at all, and I was afraid that my reputation as a scholar was at stake. Would anyone ever take my work seriously again, I wondered?

At last, tired and depressed, I invited the bear to sit down by a beautiful flower border.

We had only been
sitting for a moment
when, "Buzz! BUZZ!
BUZZZZZZZZZ!"
The loudest buzzing
I had ever heard filled
my ears. And out of
the strange *bear's* ears
flew first one and then
another big, yellow,
buzzing bee!

"What a relief!"
said the bear. "I
haven't been able to
hear a thing with
those bees buzzing
in there!"

Well, we both
rolled on the grass
laughing, and I
have tried hard
not to be such a
pompous old
bear ever
since!

The Strange Story of

THE ADVENTUROUS BEAR

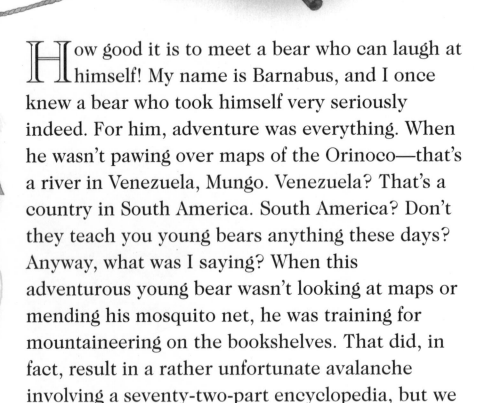

How good it is to meet a bear who can laugh at himself! My name is Barnabus, and I once knew a bear who took himself very seriously indeed. For him, adventure was everything. When he wasn't pawing over maps of the Orinoco—that's a river in Venezuela, Mungo. Venezuela? That's a country in South America. South America? Don't they teach you young bears anything these days? Anyway, what was I saying? When this adventurous young bear wasn't looking at maps or mending his mosquito net, he was training for mountaineering on the bookshelves. That did, in fact, result in a rather unfortunate avalanche involving a seventy-two-part encyclopedia, but we will pass over that.

Now, strangely enough, it was that very accident that led to the story I am about to tell you. For one of the volumes of the encyclopedia fell open at a page about a man who went around the world in eighty days. No sooner had he read this, than our friend—let's call him B.—was determined he would be the very first bear to travel right around the world.

"You will need to beware of sharks," said an old seafaring bear. "Their teeth are sharper than any bear's."

"You will have to look out for icebergs," said another bear. "And the white bears who live on them are very fierce."

"Don't forget to send us some postcards," said a little bear, who was making a collection.

B. spent months preparing for his trip. By the time he was ready, he was so loaded down with equipment, he could hardly walk.

"Good luck!" called all the bears together, as he staggered off down the path.

Well, eighty days passed. And then another eighty. There was no news from the adventurer.

"It's not surprising," said one old bear. "There are no mailboxes at all in the middle of the desert, you know."

Then, one morning, a postcard arrived. It showed a picture of the Eiffel Tower. On the back, there were just three words: *Reached France. B.*

The following month, another postcard was delivered. It showed the Leaning Tower of Pisa. The message said: *Crossing Italy. B.*

No one was very surprised when a third card arrived a few weeks later. It showed the Great Wall of China. The adventurer had written: *Learning Chinese. B.*

Next month, the excited bears waited for a postcard to drop onto the doormat. At last it came, showing a Spanish flamenco dancer. The message read: *In Spain. B.*

The young bears were dazzled by all these exotic places, but the older bears looked puzzled and shook their furry heads.

"Let me have a look at those postcards," said one. "There's something odd about our friend's route, you know."

Sure enough, when they looked closely at the postcards, everyone could see that all of them had been sent from Mountville, just a few miles away.

"I think some of us need to go on an expedition too," said the older bears.

Once again, a bear expedition was waved off from the front door, but this time, they returned before nightfall, bringing with them a very crestfallen young bear.

"I did try," he said, "but all my baggage was *so* heavy, and the world is *so* big that I came home again—only I couldn't face you all."

The oldest bear put a fatherly arm around my shoulders. "We are just happy to have you home," he said. "Come in and tell us all about your adventures."

Oh, I see that I have given the secret away. Yes, my friends, I was that foolish young bear. And I can tell you it is much better to be sitting here with you than in Turkey or Tasmania or Thailand or Timbuktu.

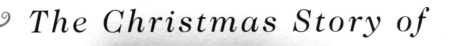

The Christmas Story of
BEARS EVERYWHERE

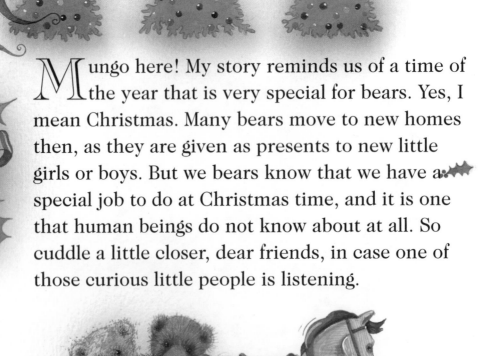

Mungo here! My story reminds us of a time of the year that is very special for bears. Yes, I mean Christmas. Many bears move to new homes then, as they are given as presents to new little girls or boys. But we bears know that we have a special job to do at Christmas time, and it is one that human beings do not know about at all. So cuddle a little closer, dear friends, in case one of those curious little people is listening.

Now, you know as well as I do that humans make a lot of mistakes. I mean the kind of mistakes that sensible bears would never make— losing their socks, tripping over their shoelaces, and forgetting each other's birthday, for example. At Christmas time they are worse than ever. Sooner or later, some silly human is likely to send the wrong present to the wrong person.

We bears, who understand how important it is to feel loved and wanted, know that someone who receives the wrong present will feel upset. Perhaps even cross. So that is why our special job at Christmas is to look out for misplaced presents and send them back to where they belong. The Teddy Bear International Mail Service was set up especially for that purpose.

One Christmas, a forgetful granny in England made a particularly bad mistake. She sent woolly gloves to her niece in Australia, where it is hot at Christmas time, and a sunhat to her niece in Canada, where the snow lay thick on the ground. And to make matters worse, she sent them at the very last minute, so it was not until the last delivery on Christmas Eve that the wrong presents arrived at the right addresses. Or the right presents arrived at the wrong addresses. You know what I mean.

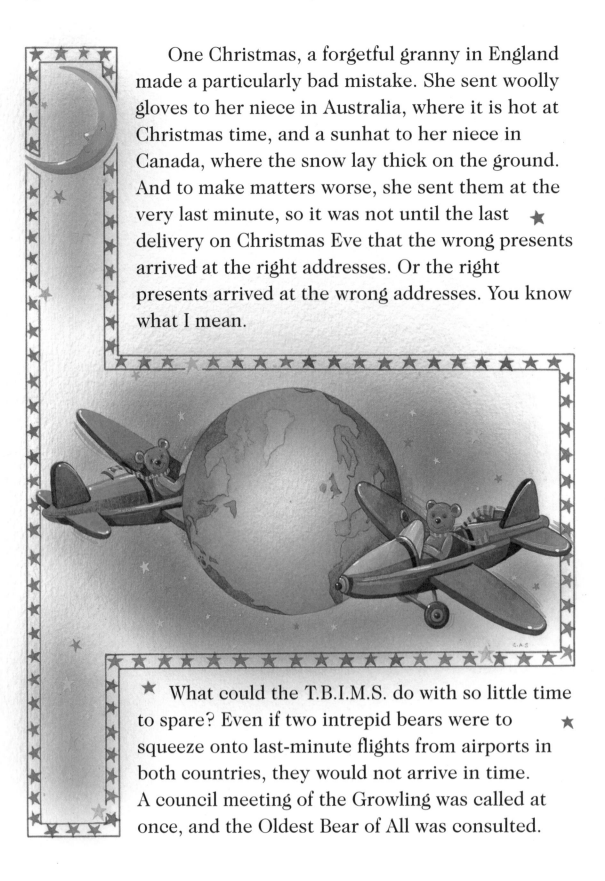

What could the T.B.I.M.S. do with so little time to spare? Even if two intrepid bears were to squeeze onto last-minute flights from airports in both countries, they would not arrive in time. A council meeting of the Growling was called at once, and the Oldest Bear of All was consulted.

"Dear bears," he said, in his quavering voice, "you have done well to bring this distressing matter to my attention. I can see only one solution, and it is one that we can use only in the most serious cases. These presents will have to be … *ahem* … lost … until Christmas is over. Please alert the bears concerned at once."

Just as soon as messages could reach the bears at opposite sides of the world, action was taken.

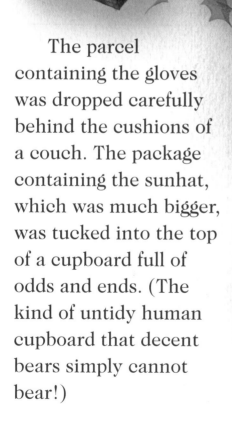

The parcel containing the gloves was dropped carefully behind the cushions of a couch. The package containing the sunhat, which was much bigger, was tucked into the top of a cupboard full of odds and ends. (The kind of untidy human cupboard that decent bears simply cannot bear!)

Now normally in this kind of situation, action is taken immediately after Christmas. The presents are exchanged and then allowed to be discovered, usually with whoops of delight, in those rather dark days after the festive season. But for some reason, both sets of bears in this case forgot all about the "missing" presents.

Yes, yes, I know. It is unpardonable. It is, as you say, Hubert, as bad as the humans themselves. Yes, I would put it that strongly. In fact, it was not until six months later that teddy bears playing on the couch in Australia discovered the offending package. In horror, they at once contacted their Canadian cousins, and that parcel was retrieved as well. Now both sets of bears were at a loss to know what to do.

The bears reported to the next meeting of the Growling as they should. There were gasps of horror around the room. Then, in the silence that followed, the Oldest Bear of All told those bears exactly what he thought of them. And it wasn't very complimentary, I can tell you.

"Sir," said one of the bears concerned, "we are more sorry than we can say. We will make the exchange at once."

But at this the Oldest Bear smiled. "I think you will find," he said, "that no exchange will now be necessary. Simply allow the presents to be found. But make sure that this NEVER happens again."

The bears were puzzled, but they did as they were told. The niece in Australia was delighted with her gloves. The niece in Canada just loved her sunhat. And both of them were pleased and puzzled to find a Christmas present so long after Christmas. Well, that puzzle is no mystery to us, my friends. But which of you clever bears can tell me why the presents did not need to be changed?

The Secret Story of

THE BEARS WHO WERE BRAVE

After that *seasonal* story, Mungo, it is my turn. My name is Bella Bear and my story tells of two bears who both did a very brave thing.

The first bear was called Walter. He was a fine bear in every way, but he had one problem. He was very, very afraid of dogs. When he was just a young bear, a visitor's poodle chewed his ears very badly indeed, and he never really got over it.

The second bear was called Hannah. She too had a great fear. She simply could not stand heights. Some bears thought that perhaps she had been dropped out of a window as a young bear. Poor Hannah could not even sit on an ordinary chair without feeling dizzy.

Both Hannah and Walter lived with a little boy called Joshua. But when Joshua's baby sister was born, Joshua said he was too old for teddy bears, and he gave Hannah and Walter to the baby. Yes, you may laugh, my friends. We know that no human is ever too old for a teddy bear.

Anyway, Joshua was a little bit upset by the amount of attention that the baby received, so his parents gave him a baby of his own—a little puppy called Jack. Jack went everywhere with Joshua, and he really was rather like a baby. He whimpered when he was hungry, and he made little puddles on the cushions, which Joshua tried to hide from the grown-ups.

One day, Hannah and Walter were left in the garden when the children were taken inside for their lunch.

Suddenly, the bears heard a frightened little bark. Somehow, the naughty puppy had managed to climb onto the roof of the summer-house. He was stuck.

"We must rescue that puppy," said Hannah.

"Why?" asked Walter.

"Because if we don't, he'll jump and hurt himself," explained his friend. "And he is a very sweet puppy."

"Hmph," said Walter.

"And Joshua loves him," Hannah added.

"All right," said Walter, "but *you* can do it, because I'm not going anywhere near him. Oh no."

"But I can't go up there!" cried Hannah. "It's much too high!"

The two little bears sat miserably looking at the puppy. Then both of them spoke at once.

"I'll go if you will," they said.

So Hannah and Walter helped each other up onto the summerhouse roof (and Hannah only had her eyes shut half the time). Then they showed the silly puppy how to get down (and Walter only hid behind Hannah because there wasn't much room to stand).

And from that day to this, none of the humans in the house know how brave the little bears were. But the puppy knew, and I think he told Joshua, because a few days later, the little boy decided that his sister was too *small* for teddy bears, and he tucked Hannah and Walter into *his* bed again. Which is how it should be, after all.

The Sleepy Story of
THE BEAR WHO COULDN'T STAY AWAKE

My friends, the fire is burning low and the smallest bears have fallen asleep on our laps. Perhaps we should all go off to bed now. What? One more story? Well, if you are sure.

My story is of a very sleepy bear called Selina. Whenever she was wanted, Selina was always to be found dozing in a corner. Some bears were rather suspicious about Selina's sleeping. Somehow, when there was a treat in store, such as extra honey or a birthday party, Selina was always awake. When there was tidying to be done, or muddy pawprints to be removed, or honeypots to wash, Selina would be snoring quietly somewhere.

"If you ask me," grumbled the Oldest Bear of All, "that lazy little bear is just pretending. She needs to be taught a lesson."

"Bears do need their sleep," explained her friend Marilyn anxiously. "Selina would be so upset if she knew what horrible things were being said about her. And she has slept right through suppertime. She wouldn't do that if she was really awake. She's always very hungry."

At that moment, Selina gave an extra loud snore.

The older bears shook their heads. "If she is pretending," they said, "she will wake up after we are asleep and have a little snack then. What we must do is stay awake tonight and watch carefully to see what happens."

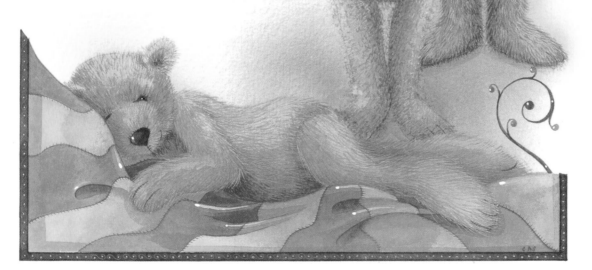

So five bears volunteered not to go to bed. As it grew dark, they took up their positions and watched the sleeping Selina.

Very soon, the first little bear's nose began to twitch. He was trying to stop himself from yawning. Then his bright little eyes began to close. In just two minutes, he was fast asleep.

The second little bear struggled hard to stay awake. He patted his head with his paws to stop himself from drifting off to sleep. But his patting grew slower, and slower, and slower … until he too was dreaming a teddy-bear dream.

The third bear was older than the first two. He was quite determined to stay awake. He decided to march up and down—quietly, of course. *Pad, pad, pad,* he marched across the floor. *Pad, pad, pad,* back he came. *Pad, pad, pad … pad, pad, pad.* He looked as if he was awake. He sounded as if he was awake. But before long, that bear was sleep-walking! His eyes were closed, but his little legs were still moving. In his furry head, he dreamed of being a soldier on parade.

★ The fourth and fifth watching bears decided to keep each other awake. They talked in whispers late into the night. But there is something very soft and sleepy about whispering. Although they tried hard to stay awake, soon the whispers became gentle snores.

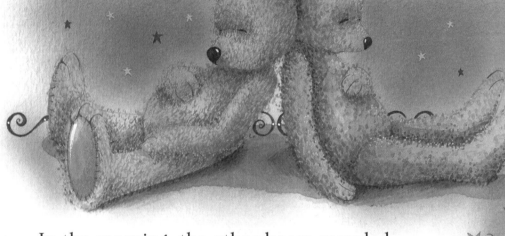

In the morning, the other bears crowded round to see what had happened.

"Well … *ahem*," said the first bear, "I certainly didn't see her wake up." ★

"Er … neither did I," agreed the second bear.

"I was on duty all night," said the third bear, "and I didn't hear a sound."

The fourth and fifth bears looked at each other, and scratched their furry heads. "I saw nothing unusual," said one, truthfully. "Did you, old pal?"

"Nothing at all," replied his friend firmly.

So the mystery of the sleeping bear never was solved. But Selina, who was sleeping happily in her usual place, gave an extra loud snore and the tiniest, sleepy, secret smile.

Now it is time for little bears everywhere to go to sleep. Goodnight, little bears! Goodnight!

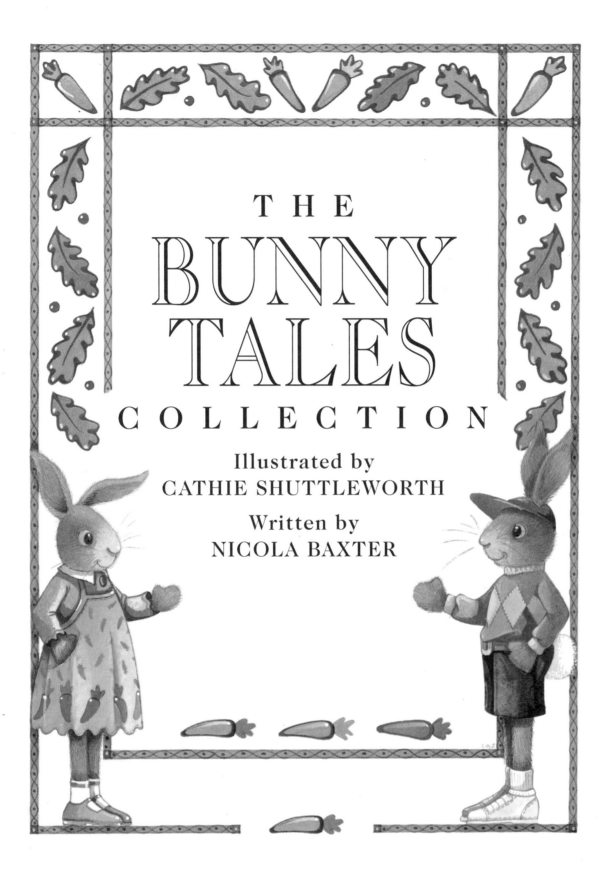

THE
BUNNY
TALES
COLLECTION

Illustrated by
CATHIE SHUTTLEWORTH

Written by
NICOLA BAXTER

Great-Uncle Otto's Tale of
THE BIG BAD BUNNY

One morning, the little bunnies were being unusually annoying. When they bounced on Great Uncle Otto's chair and broke the springs, that very wise old rabbit sighed and decided enough was well and truly enough.

"You young bunnies should be careful," he warned, waving his willow walking stick. "If you're not careful, you'll find yourselves in a very sticky situation indeed, just like the Big Bad Bunny."

"Oh, tell us, tell us!" called Pickles and Penny and all the other little bunnies.

"Very well," said Great-Uncle Otto, "but first you must find a cushion to put in my poor old chair and then you must sit absolutely still."

The little rabbits hurried to get ready. They loved the old rabbit's stories.

"The big bad bunny," Great-Uncle Otto began, "was once just an ordinary naughty little bunny—like you!"

The little bunnies wriggled in their seats, and Great-Uncle Otto went on.

"As this particular naughty bunny got older," he said, "he also got bigger and badder, until he was a very big, very bad bunny indeed."

"What did he do?" squealed Pickles.

"He tied his sister's shoelaces together, so she fell over. He ate his brother's birthday cake *before* that poor little bunny's birthday. He shut his mother in the pantry while he made mud pies on the living room carpet. He put jelly in his father's slippers. He gathered a bunch of flowers for his auntie . . . from her own garden. He filled the bathtub with frogs and put worms in the kitchen sink. Need I say more?"

"Oooh!" said the little bunnies. "He *was* bad, wasn't he?"

"He was," said Great-Uncle Otto gravely, "but, as I said, he found himself in a sticky situation. Oh yes, a very sticky situation indeed."

"What happened?" squeaked Penny.

"Honey," replied her great-uncle briefly.

"Honey?"

"Yes, honey. One day, his mother left a big jar of honey on the table when she went shopping. Of course, the big bad bunny wanted to taste it. He dipped in one paw. Then that greedy bunny dipped in two paws. But, you know, that honey was very thick and gloopy. He found that his paws were completely stuck!

And when he bent his head to try to pull out his paws, his ears got stuck to the sticky jar as well! Of course, he struggled, and when his mother came home, she found him with the jar on his head and one ear and two paws stuck inside it, while gloopy, golden honey trickled slowly down his face. He was not a happy bunny."

"And was he good after that?" asked Pickles.

"He was," said Great-Uncle Otto firmly. "He became a fine, upstanding bunny, kind, er . . . wise, and respected by all. Now run along and play and let me read my book."

"What was the big bad bunny's name?" asked Penny, as the little bunnies ran out of the door.

"Hrrrmph!" grunted her great-uncle. "Well, he happened to be called . . . *ahem* . . . Otto!"

Aunt Amelia's Tale of

The Funny Bunny

Rain was falling steadily in Warren Wood. The little bunnies looked miserably at the puddles forming near the entrance to the burrow. There would be no playing outside today.

"What can we do?" asked Whistler. "Hide and seek? Chase the bunny? I-spy?"

"Oh no," groaned Merry, "we've played those hundreds of times. We could tell jokes, though."

"I don't know any jokes," grumbled Pickles.

"Don't you?" said an amused voice from behind the sofa. It was Aunt Amelia, who had been picking up the tiny bits of thread she had dropped when she was doing her embroidery. "I know lots of jokes," said the surprising aunt. "They were told to me by a very funny bunny. He made everyone laugh so much that their ears went wobbly. I still know lots of his jokes."

"Like what?" asked Penny, suspiciously. In her experience, a grown-up rabbit's idea of what was funny was often very odd.

"Er . . . well, did you hear about the bunny who chopped down a tree, sawed it up, and made a car out of it?"

"No," said Pickles slowly.

"It wooden go!" chortled Aunt Amelia.

"Why not?" asked Penny.

"No, no, you don't understand!" cried her aunt. "The car was made of *wood* and it *wooden* go!"

A deafening silence greeted this statement. Clearly, the little bunnies didn't think it was funny at all.

"All right," said Aunt Amelia, searching her memory for another good joke. "Here's one. How can you tell if there's an elephant in a cupboard?"

"What's an efelant?" asked baby Bubbles.

Once this was explained, Aunt Amelia started her joke all over again. She sensed that her very best jokes were not going as well as she had hoped.

"I don't know," sighed Pickles. "How can you tell if there's an elephant in a cupboard?"

"Ha ha! Because the door won't shut!" crowed Aunt Amelia, her face quite pink with giggling.

The little bunnies looked at each other. This was really dreadful. But there was no stopping the embarrassing aunt.

"What do you give a sick bird?"

"What sort of bird?" asked Whistler.

"It doesn't matter what sort of bird." Aunt Amelia was beginning to get tetchy.

"Could it be a duck?"

"No, it couldn't be a duck, but it could be any kind of small bird."

"Why is it sick?" asked baby Bubbles.

"I don't know why it's sick," said Aunt Amelia faintly, "but what would you give it, anyway?"

"That depends on why it was sick," explained Penny. "If it had eaten too much, you wouldn't give it food, but if it hadn't eaten for days, you would, you see."

But Aunt Amelia was already halfway out of the room. ★

"I can see that the funny bunny's jokes are too sophisticated for you little ones," she sniffed. "I'm going to lie down." ★

When she had gone, the little bunnies forgot all about the jokes and had a lively game of hip-hop-ho until it was time for supper and bed.

So no one realized just why it was that baby Bubbles woke up the next morning with a smile all over his face, saying, "Tweetment!"

Father Rabbit's Tale of
THE
CARROT COLLECTION

Tempers in the Big Burrow became a little
frayed when Penny and Pickles started
collecting things. They had a friend who collected
postcards, but they thought that was pretty
boring. Both of them wanted to collect something
much more exciting than that.

"I'm going to collect leaves," said Penny.
"They're really interesting, and there are lots of
different kinds."

"I'm going to collect caterpillars," said Pickles. "There are lots of different kinds of them too, and they can crawl, you know, which is much, much more exciting."

"Hmmm," Penny was not so sure. Dimly in the back of her mind, she felt that there might be a problem if lots of caterpillars started crawling around in the Big Burrow. But it was impossible to change Pickles' mind once he had decided on something. Before long, every corner of his bedroom was filled with little jars and pots, covered with paper lids in which Pickles had carefully punched little holes.

"I hope you're giving those caterpillars plenty to eat," said Father Rabbit, looking suspiciously at the jars. "Caterpillars who are hungry might have a tendency to roam."

But Pickles took very good care of his caterpillars. In fact, he was so interested in them that he didn't even notice what Penny was doing.

Unfortunately, the day came when it was raining so hard that Pickles couldn't go outside to find leaves for his creepy-crawly friends. He was beginning to get desperate when he noticed a pile of leaves in the corner of the hallway outside the dining room.

"Those will be fine," said Pickles.

It was not until that evening, when Pickles' caterpillars had done quite a bit of chomping and chewing, that Penny was heard to shout from the middle of the burrow, "Who's moved my leaf collection?" Pickles hid under the bed for a very long time.

Next morning, it seemed that Pickles, too, had troubles. Each one of his caterpillars had turned into a hard, shiny thing that didn't move at all. Pickles left all his jars open in disgust.

"I can't understand you young rabbits," said Father Rabbit, when he saw the two little ones sitting sadly on the stairs. "In my day we used to collect something useful . . . like carrots! Why, I remember having the biggest and best carrot collection in all of Warren Wood. Let me tell you about it. Storage was the biggest problem, but I had a clever idea. . . ."

Now this was not the first time that the little
rabbits had heard about Father Rabbit's famous
carrot collection, and they were very sorry indeed
that they'd given him the opportunity to tell them
about it all over again. There were even
photographs of the collection, which he eagerly
dug out of a drawer. Between you and me, there
are few things more boring than photographs of
carrots, especially photographs of *hundreds* of
carrots in rows. The carrot stories went on for days.

Finally, the little rabbits could stand it no
longer. "Er . . . I must go and clear up my
bedroom," said Pickles, which was such an
unusual thing for him to say that Penny fell off her
chair in surprise. But when she had picked herself
up, she half remembered that she had promised to
help Pickles, and she hurried off to join him.

And when the rabbits opened the door of Pickles' bedroom, they had the most wonderful surprise. Every one of the hard, shiny things had hatched . . .

into a beautiful, fluttering butterfly.

Grandma Molly's Tale of

THE TREETOP BUNNY

The annoying thing about kites is that they have a habit of getting stuck in trees. One breezy spring day, Penny and Pickles were as careful as they could be with their new kite. But when your mother has told you not to go very far from home, and your home is under a tree, accidents are bound to happen. Before long, the kite was hopelessly tangled, high in the branches.

Pickles at once tried to climb up to reach the balloon. But bunnies are not very good at climbing. He was only a little way from the ground before he too got stuck.

When Grandma Molly came out for some fresh air, she was surprised to see a kite *and* a rabbit dangling from different branches.

"Why, don't tell me you're going to take after your great-great-great-great-uncle Ebenezer, Pickles!" she cried.

Pickles was so
interested in the idea of
a great-great-great-
great-uncle that he
forgot to hold on and
came down to earth
with a *bump!*

"Who was *he*?"
asked the little bunny,
rubbing his bottom.

"I'll tell you about
him," said Grandma
Molly, "to take your
mind off your . . . er . . .
unmentionable bits."

Penny and Pickles
giggled, but they settled
down to hear the story.

"Ebenezer," said Grandma, "was a very strange
bunny. He always wanted to be somewhere *high*.
When he was a tiny baby, he would try to climb up
onto the table. When he was older, he would
balance on the tops of doors. *Very* dangerous. And
when he was older still, he realized that trees were
the tallest things around, and he wanted more
than anything to go to live in a house at the top of
a tree."

"But only birds live in trees!" said Penny.

"And bees," Pickles reminded her. He had had
a rather painful experience the year before.

"Yes, indeed," replied Grandma Molly, "but that didn't stop Ebenezer. He tried to climb every tree he could. Unfortunately, as you've found, Pickles, bunnies are not good at climbing trees. They're very good at jumping but not very good at climbing. Even Ebenezer, who had had a lot of practice, found it difficult."

"What did he do?" breathed Penny.

"He didn't know what to do," said Grandma, "until his little cousin had a birthday party. One of the little bunnies was almost carried away by a balloon. Then Ebenezer knew how to get to the top of the tree."

"With a balloon?"

"Well, he needed more than one balloon, of course, but yes, that was his idea. That very afternoon, Ebenezer held onto a huge bunch of balloons and floated into the air. Up, up, up he went until. . ."

"Yes?" said Pickles.

"Yes?" cried Penny.

"The balloons touched the leaves of the tree."

"That didn't matter, did it?" asked Pickles, looking at the smooth edge of a leaf that had been stuck in his ears.

"Ah," said Grandma, "but this was not an oak tree, or an ash, or a maple. It was a holly tree!"

"They have really sharp leaves," squeaked Penny.

"*Pop! Pop! Pop! Pop!* The balloons burst one by one, and Ebenezer fell with a *bump!* onto a broad branch."

"How did he get down?" asked Pickles, thinking of his own painful fall.

"He didn't," said Grandma. "He liked it so much that he stayed up there. You know, sometimes when I catch sight of those mischievous little animals called squirrels, I can't help wondering if they are related to old Ebenezer."

Can you see some squirrels watching Penny and Pickles right now, high up in the branches? What do you think?

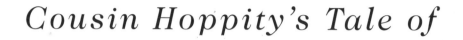

Cousin Hoppity's Tale of

THE BEST BIRTHDAY

When it was almost time for Pickles' birthday, nobody had any peace. Pickles was determined to have the biggest and best birthday that had ever been seen in Warren Wood. But what should it be like? Ever since he had been to Billy Bunny's Pirate Party, Pickles felt that a party should have a theme. He just couldn't decide what his should be.

"How about Dragons and Princesses?" said Penny, who liked the idea of dressing up as a beautiful princess.

"I don't want to be a dragon," said Pickles.

"How about Fairies and Elves?" suggested Penny. A fairy costume would be good, too.

"My ears are big enough, without pretending to be an elf," replied Pickles. "And anyway, Jimble already had one of those for his birthday last year. It would look as if I was copying."

Every day, Pickles worried about his party.

He was still worrying a few days later, when Cousin Hoppity came to stay.

Cousin Hoppity lived in a wood that was even wilder than Warren Wood and had a large river flowing through it. He was always full of stories of the adventures he had had. Pickles was secretly envious of him, but he always pretended to enjoy the calmer life under the oak tree.

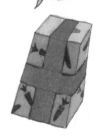
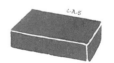

"When it comes to birthdays," said Cousin Hoppity, "I'm the rabbit you want to ask. On my very best birthday, I didn't even *have* a party."

Despite himself, Pickles heard his own voice asking to hear the story. Hoppity was only too glad to begin.

"My birthday is in the spring," he said, "when the river is always high and fast-flowing. Last year, it rained for days and days and days. On the morning of my birthday, I woke up to a splashing sound."

"Rain on the window?" asked Pickles in a bored voice.

"Water on the window, certainly," said Hoppity, "but it was lapping at the panes, not falling on them. The whole wood was flooded, right up to the second branch of our tree."

Penny was horrified. "What about all the poor rabbits underground?" she cried.

"Rabbits in Wilderness Wood are sensible and strong," said Hoppity. "They had all climbed up into the trunk of the tree and were busy making little boats out of everything they could find. As I looked out of the window, my great-grandmother sailed past in a suitcase. She had made a sail out of an old pair of her . . . *ahem*, well, bloomers."

The little rabbits giggled at the idea, but Pickles had more questions.

"What happened to all your presents?" he asked. He was thinking about the interesting packages that he knew were hiding under his parents' bed at that very moment.

"Luckily," said Hoppity, "they were the kind of presents that float. One by one, they came floating past my window, and I fished them out with my fishing rod. It was loads of fun, even if some of them were pretty soggy for a while. And my birthday cake never was seen again."

"I can see that it was exciting," said Pickles. "But why was it the best birthday ever?"

"Because of the whale," cried Hoppity, stretching his paws out wide. "A great big whale swam up the river and into the wood, and it got stuck between two trees."

Pickles was almost speechless. "A w-w-whale?" he gasped. "In Wilderness Wood? What happened to it?"

"We all made boats of everything we could find," said Hoppity, "as I explained. Then we sailed out and attached ropes to the whale. It was a tough job, but at last we managed to pull him out from between the trees and tow him back to the river and, eventually, the sea. It was the adventure of a lifetime, I can assure you. I can't imagine that

anything as exciting as that happens in Warren Wood, does it?"

Pickles and Penny were silent. Nothing they had ever heard of even came close. It made the Party Problem seem pathetically small.

It was only later that night that Pickles began to think hard about that whale.

Next morning, he tackled Hoppity.

"There wasn't really a whale, was there?" he asked with a smile.

"Of course not," laughed Hoppity, "but it was a really good story, wasn't it? Now, what about a Deep Sea Party for your birthday?"

Pickles had to admit that was a pretty good idea. And Penny was as happy as could be, as she planned her mermaid costume.

Sister Susie-Sally's Tale of

THE FRIENDLY FOX

Pickles' big sister Susie-Sally was grown-up. She lived in a burrow on the other side of Warren Wood with her husband's family and her own baby rabbits. One afternoon, she came to visit her father and mother and to say hello to her baby brother. She found him playing in a clearing near the edge of the wood.

"Hello, Susa," called Pickles. When he was little, he couldn't say her full name, and his pet name for her had stuck.

Susie-Sally took her new responsibilities as a parent very seriously.

"Are you sure you should be playing all by yourself, young Pickles?" she asked. "You never know who might be lurking between the trees. What if there was a fox?"

"There hasn't been a fox in Warren Wood for ever so long," said Pickles, "and anyway, I don't think foxes are as bad as old rabbits say they are. I think they're like ogres and giants and goblins— they only really live in stories."

"I see," said his big sister. "Well, shall I tell you a story about a fox—a friendly fox?"

So as Susie-Sally led Pickles back to his home under the old oak tree, this is the story she told him.

"Once upon a time," she said, "there was a little rabbit who wouldn't do what his mother told him. He always had to find out for himself. If she told him not to touch a saucepan because it was hot, he would touch it anyway and burn his paws. When she told him not to go near the river, in case he fell in, he ran right to the edge of the bank and, of course . . . *splash!* . . . he was up to his ears in water. Luckily, two grown-up rabbits who were fishing nearby scooped him out—just in time."

Susie-Sally paused for breath. She could see that Pickles was listening intently.

"One day," she went on, "the little rabbit's mother told him to play indoors and, no matter what, not to wander out into the Wild Wood."

"But he did," Pickles squealed, "didn't he?"

"He did," said Susie-Sally solemnly, "and there he met a very friendly fox."

"I knew foxes were friendly," Pickles said. "What happened?"

"The fox was so friendly," said his big sister, "that he invited the little rabbit to see his den. That is what foxes call their homes, you know. They live underground, like us, though their rooms are not nearly as nice and they are not very good at housekeeping."

"Did he go?" asked Pickles. "The little rabbit, I mean. Did he go to the fox's den?"

"Yes, he went right along, and as the two of them trotted through the wood, the fox said, 'I especially wanted you to come for supper today. My family is really looking forward to it. Such a treat!'"

"How nice of the fox," said Pickles. "I wish I could meet him and visit his den."

"Not so fast, young Pickles. Wait till I tell you what happened to that little rabbit. He arrived at the fox's den and went inside. There were two little baby foxes there and a mother fox. And all of them smiled the biggest, toothiest smiles you have ever seen when they looked at the plump little rabbit. They were all just as friendly as the father fox had been."

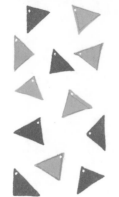

"Did they play games?" asked Pickles.

"Yes, they played foxy games. They played Pounce and Push and they played Chase the Bunny and they played Catch."

"Those sound like good games," said Pickles.

"They were good games for foxes," agreed Susie-Sally darkly.

"So then they had supper?" asked her little brother. "What did they have for supper?"

"I hope you won't be upset, Pickles, but it was a tasty pie, made of something plump and furry."

Pickles was very quiet as they walked on.

"I know I shouldn't ask," he said at last. "But was it . . . I mean, it wasn't. . . . That is, you're not saying . . . are you?"

"I'm saying," said his sister, "that you should *always* do what your mother and father tell you, and you shouldn't trust strangers, no matter how friendly they seem. And more than that, I don't think I need to say. Do I?"

"No," agreed Pickles hastily. "You don't need to say anything else at all. I think I might play nearer home from now on. I must keep an eye on the younger rabbits, after all."

Mother Rabbit's Tale of
Too Much Fudge

One afternoon, Pickles and Penny didn't feel very well. In fact, they felt so sick that their ears and whiskers drooped and they went to bed— while the sun was still shining.

Mother Rabbit was worried about her little ones. She asked them all kinds of questions about what might be wrong.

"Have you got colds?" she inquired. "Are there sniffles in your noses?"

"No, Mother," groaned Pickles.

"Did you play in the hot sun without your hats on? Are your ears aching?"

"No, Mother," moaned Penny.

"I may have to call Doctor Baggins," said Mother, "if you two don't feel better soon. I'll just go and get you each a glass of water."

But in the kitchen, Mother Rabbit saw something that made her change her mind about calling the doctor, and she didn't look quite so worried when she went back to the little rabbits.

"I'll just sit here and tell you a story," said Mother Rabbit, "and you can go to sleep and feel much better when you wake up."

"Once upon a time," said Mother Rabbit, "there were two little rabbits who always did what their mother told them. They were as good as gold. They wouldn't dream of hiding under the bed when it was time to wash the dishes. They always squeezed the toothpaste from the end of the tube. They never left dirty pawmarks in the bathroom. It was always a pleasure for their mother to look at her two little rabbits and say, 'My children are not silly like other bunnies. They are good, sensible young rabbits.'"

While Mother Rabbit was talking, quite a bit of wriggling and jiggling could be heard coming from two little bunnies in bed. Mother Rabbit smiled grimly.

"One day," she went on, "the little rabbits' mother was very busy in the kitchen. There was a Grand Fair the next day, and she had promised to bake some cakes for the cake stall. But when she looked in her cupboard, she found that she didn't have any eggs. She had no time to run out and buy some more, so she looked at the ingredients she did have to see if there was something else she could make. Pretty soon, she was melting all kinds of good things in a pan. A lovely smell came out of the kitchen, so that the two little rabbits came to see what was being cooked. The mother rabbit was stirring something with a big wooden spoon.

'This fudge isn't for you!' she laughed."

At that point, Mother Rabbit heard some shuffling and snuffling from her little rabbits. She smoothed down her apron and prepared to finish her story.

"By lunchtime," she said, "the mother rabbit had filled ten large tins with hot fudge. She put the pans on the kitchen table to cool. Of course, she knew that her little ones would never dream of tasting the delicious fudge. They knew that they must not eat sweet, sticky things between meals. So you can imagine how surprised she was when she came back from hanging out the laundry to find that two of the pans of fudge were missing. Obviously, she thought, someone had believed that she would not be able to count so many pans and might not notice that some were gone."

Now there was a deep silence from the two little rabbits. Mother Rabbit decided it was time to finish her story.

"Of course," she said, "it was very easy for the mother rabbit to find out who had stolen the fudge. Any rabbit would feel ill after eating a whole pan of sweet, sticky stuff. All she had to do was to visit all her friends and see who was looking a bit green around the whiskers. By the way, how are you two little bunnies feeling now? Any better? Or do I need to call Dr. Baggins?"

"No, no," cried Pickles and Penny, creeping out of their beds. "There's nothing wrong with us at all now. We feel fine!"

But you know, it's a strange thing, neither of those two little rabbits wanted anything for supper!

Half-Cousin Colly's Tale of

THE GHASTLY GHOST

Bunnies love to live together in big families. It doesn't matter how many brothers and sisters, aunts and uncles, cousins and half-cousins come along, there is always room for them. When everyone is starting to feel a little crowded, some grown-up rabbits just dig another couple of rooms so that all the bunnies can breathe again.

Bunnies enjoy living together so much that they don't usually feel the need to get away from it all, but they do love to visit their relatives in other burrows. One day, Pickles and his mother went to visit Half-Cousin Colly, who lived in a very ancient burrow under a wild, open heath. Pickles asked his mother to explain what a half-cousin was, but even after she had told him, he couldn't figure it out. All he knew was that Colly was a grown-up rabbit and he had once heard his granny say that he was eccentric. Pickles really didn't know what that meant either, so he had very little idea of what to expect.

The journey seemed to take forever.

It was growing dark when Pickles and his mother reached the entrance to Half-Cousin Colly's home. They decided at once that there was only one word to describe it. It was *spooky*.

"Why are there so many cobwebs?" whispered Pickles, clutching his mother's paw.

"Because there are so many spiders," said Mother Rabbit quietly. "Come on."

Mamma rang the bell, which clanged so loudly that Pickles, who was already feeling a little nervous, almost jumped out of his skin. The door opened with an ominous creak—all by itself! The two rabbits went in.

As the two bunnies walked slowly into the hallway, they suddenly felt very cold.

"I don't like it," wailed Pickles, burying his face in his mother's skirt. "It's scary!"

But just then, a cheerful voice called from a nearby room.

"Come on in, my dears! How lovely to see you!"

A jolly, plump rabbit in a bright red robe came towards them. It was Half-Cousin Colly.

After a delicious supper and lots of talk about family and friends, Pickles felt much better. Half-Cousin Colly was a friendly rabbit with lots of good stories to tell. Pickles forgot that he had ever been frightened in the large burrow.

But when it was time to go to bed, Colly showed Pickles to an enormous room with a big four-poster bed. The minute Colly shut the door with a cheery "Good night!" Pickles began to feel scared again.

Pickles lay awake in the silence, listening to his heart going *thump, thump, thump* in the darkness. It was not very long before he crept out of the room and slipped into his mother's bed, where it was warm and snug and safe.

"I know, Pickles," whispered Mother Rabbit, as she cuddled him. "There's something strange about this house. I'm just not quite sure what it is."

Next morning, the two bunnies met Half-Cousin Colly for breakfast. Mother Rabbit, who believed in sorting things out as soon as possible, spoke her mind.

"Colly," she said, "I'm afraid that both Pickles and I have felt uncomfortable in this house ever since we arrived. Is there something about it that you should tell us? It's almost as if it was . . . well, I don't like to say this, but . . . haunted."

Pickles almost fell off his chair when Half-Cousin Colly answered sadly, "Yes, this house is haunted. I share it with a ghastly ghost, and I suppose I should tell you about it."

"Is it a story suitable for a young bunny?" asked Mother Rabbit, preparing to cover Pickles' ears with her paws.

"It's something that every young bunny should know about," said Colly firmly. "There is a ghastly ghost that haunts every single part of this house. It is here all the time, day and night, but it is especially noticeable in the middle of the night. I have become so used to it that I hardly notice anymore. It is only when friends come to stay that I can see how uncomfortable they feel about it."

"Then you must do something about it," said Mother Rabbit briskly. "Ghosts can be dealt with, you know. Your home used to be so warm and inviting, full of laughing bunnies and. . ." Mother Rabbit broke off as she began to realize what Colly meant.

Half-Cousin Colly nodded his head. "I can see that you understand, my dear," he said. "The name of my ghastly ghost is loneliness. Since my wife passed away and my little ones went to homes of their own, this burrow has been so silent and lonely. It is far too big a burrow for one bunny like me, yet I cannot bring myself to leave the home where we once all lived so happily together."

"I think I have an idea," said Mother Rabbit with a smile. "Why not have other rabbits to stay? You are a wonderful cook and would make everyone so welcome. Rabbits on their way to another place or rabbits who wanted a break from their usual burrows would love to come, I'm sure."

And that is why, if you visit Half-Cousin Colly's Bunny Bed and Breakfast today (though I hear he is booked up months ahead!) you will find a very different kind of burrow. And as for the loneliness ghost, it has gone right away, and that is the only guest that Half-Cousin Colly *won't* be inviting back!

Aunt Prettypaws' Tale of

RIBBONS AND LACE

One day you may be lucky enough to get an invitation to a bunny wedding. If you do, please, *please* accept it, for no one knows how to celebrate like bunnies do. They will throw a party for any tiny thing, so you can imagine that a wedding is a very big event. The singing, dancing, feasting, and fun go on for days and days.

Although Pickles and Penny loved to go and join in the merrymaking, they were not very interested in hearing stories about weddings. There is always a lot to organize when two bunnies get married, and the little rabbits knew that elderly aunts in particular just love to tell you all about the hundreds of weddings they have helped to make occasions to remember.

Aunt Prettypaws was like that. She didn't visit very often, but when she did she was always busy embroidering some frilly scrap of material or threading ribbons through a wedding shawl. When Aunt Prettypaws was around, Pickles and Penny often tried not to be!

But one morning, when the snow was too deep on the ground for little bunnies to hop, Pickles and Penny found themselves shut up in the living room with Aunt Prettypaws.

Penny untangled a bag of ribbon for the old bunny, while Pickles found that it was fun to look through Aunt Prettypaws' workbag. And that is how they came to hear the tale of ribbons and lace.

"I'm sure you know, young bunnies," Aunt Prettypaws began, "that it is the custom for bunny brides to make their own wedding dresses. And the days are long gone when a simple gown would do. Oh no, nowadays brides must wear as many ribbons and frills as they can."

"My cousin Mabel could hardly move," said Penny, remembering how she had had to help to push the bride through a narrow doorway, tucking her frilly skirts around her.

"Well, that is probably going too far," smiled Aunt Prettypaws. "But the bride I am thinking of almost didn't go far enough."

"What happened?" asked Penny.

"Well, Letitia was a lovely young bunny in every way, but she was always busy. She looked after baby bunnies in the mornings. She helped her father in his digging business in the afternoons. And in between, she was the leading light of most of the clubs and societies in Warren Wood. And that is why, I'm sorry to say, she put off making her wedding dress until the very, very, last moment."

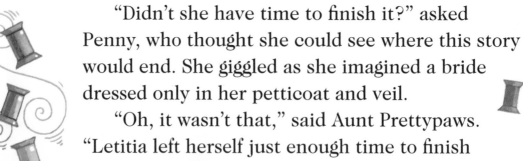

"Didn't she have time to finish it?" asked Penny, who thought she could see where this story would end. She giggled as she imagined a bride dressed only in her petticoat and veil.

"Oh, it wasn't that," said Aunt Prettypaws. "Letitia left herself just enough time to finish sewing the dress. No, her problem came when she went to old Mr. Bobbin's shop to buy her ribbons and lace. For the shop was closed, and a big sign on the door said 'AWAY ON BUSINESS. BACK NEXT MONTH.'"

"So she had no ribbons and no lace?" asked Pickles, winding some ribbon around his paws. "What did she do next, Auntie?"

"She cried," sighed Aunt Prettypaws. "Yes, she sat down on a tree stump in Warren Wood and sobbed. She thought her wedding dress would be ruined, and she had so wanted to look lovely on her special day. But as she sat there, her old granny happened to come along."

"Did she have some ribbons and lace?" asked Penny.

"No," said Aunt Prettypaws, "but she had a very good idea. She told Letitia not to worry and went off to see her friends deep in the wood. She knew they would help."

"Did they have a shop too?" asked Pickles.

"No, they were not bunnies at all. They were little woodland creatures so tiny you often don't even see them as you walk by their workshops. Yes, Granny went to talk to the spiders, who can spin lace so fine and beautiful that no bunny can match it. Then she visited the little birds who hop along the hedges. She had a special job for them, you see."

"For a whole week, the spiders were spinning their delicate lace and the little birds were gathering rose petals and threading them together to make long pink ribbons. Then they carried the lovely things they had made to Granny."

"Was there time to sew them all onto the dress?" asked Penny, who found that sewing took a long time.

"There was just enough time," smiled Aunt Prettypaws, "and everyone said that Letitia's dress was the prettiest they had ever seen."

"I'd like my wedding dress to have spider lace and rose-petal ribbons," sighed Penny, which made Pickles groan and hide his head in Aunt Prettypaws' workbag!

Baby Honeybun's Tale of
THE TALKING TOY

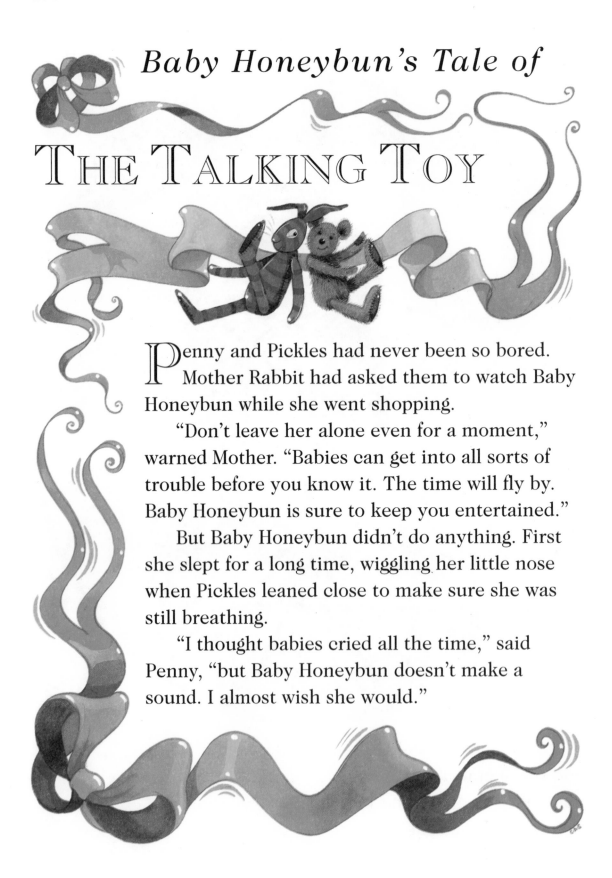

Penny and Pickles had never been so bored. Mother Rabbit had asked them to watch Baby Honeybun while she went shopping.

"Don't leave her alone even for a moment," warned Mother. "Babies can get into all sorts of trouble before you know it. The time will fly by. Baby Honeybun is sure to keep you entertained."

But Baby Honeybun didn't do anything. First she slept for a long time, wiggling her little nose when Pickles leaned close to make sure she was still breathing.

"I thought babies cried all the time," said Penny, "but Baby Honeybun doesn't make a sound. I almost wish she would."

As if she had heard Penny, Baby Honeybun suddenly woke up and gave two big sneezes. They were such large sneezes coming from a tiny bunny that even Baby Honeybun herself looked shocked and shook her little whiskers to and fro.

"Maybe now she'll play with us," said Pickles. "Here, Baby! Chase Uncle Pickles!"

But Baby Honeybun just sat looking up at Pickles. She didn't move at all.

"Can she walk?" asked Pickles.

"I don't think so." Penny shook her head. "But I think she can roll around on her tummy."

"Well, she's not doing it now," said Pickles. "She's not doing anything at all. I didn't realize that babies were so *boring*. I bet I wasn't like this when I was little. Do something, Baby!"

Baby Honeybun blinked. She wiggled her nose. She gave a big sigh. And she went straight back to sleep, snuggled into a cushion on the floor.

Now anyone who has ever looked after a bunny baby—or any baby, for that matter—for any length of time will know that sleeping is a Good Thing. While a baby is sleeping, she isn't crawling into the coal scuttle or pulling off her clothes or doing any one of the hundreds of things that babies do so well.

But Penny didn't know much about babies, and that is why she made a Really Big Mistake. She nudged Baby Honeybun's toe to wake her up.

Baby Honeybun stirred, as though she didn't quite believe what she had felt.

Penny nudged her gently again.

Baby Honeybun opened one eye. There was no doubt about it.

She looked angry. In fact, she looked angrier than any baby bunny Pickles and Penny had ever seen. Then Baby Honeybun opened her little pink mouth and began to yell.

It wasn't a quiet, unhappy kind of yell. It wasn't a medium-sized, slightly annoyed kind of yell. It was a huge, I-am-furious kind of yell, and it didn't stop.

Baby Honeybun yelled and yelled and yelled. Her little face grew pinker and pinker, and tiny tears ran down her furry cheeks.

"What should I do?" cried Penny. "I didn't mean to upset her!"

"Maybe she's hungry," suggested Pickles. "We could give her some milk." He always found a snack was helpful in a crisis.

"No, no," cried Penny. "She has a special kind and I don't know where it is. We don't want to poison her, too!"

"We could pick her up and cuddle her," suggested Pickles.

"You try," said Penny. "I'm not going to touch her again. Look what happened last time."

Very, very carefully, Pickles picked up the screaming baby. She was surprisingly heavy.

"Ouch!" yelled Pickles. And he put the baby back onto her cushion as quickly as he could. "She kicked me!" he squealed.

"We'll have to try singing," said Penny. And she launched into a rousing chorus of "Five Little Bunnies" before Pickles could stop her.

It didn't seem possible that Baby Honeybun could yell any louder, but she did. At the sound of the song, she made an extra-special effort, and her pink face went purple with rage.

Penny was almost in tears herself now. But she had no more ideas.

"We could tell her a story," said Pickles. "Once upon a time, there was a little baby bunny called Baby Honeybun. . . ."

Baby Honeybun's yells became a tiny fraction quieter.

". . .she lived in a burrow with her two best friends, Penny and Pickles," Penny went on.

Baby Honeybun's yells increased again.

"No, no, she didn't," said Pickles hastily. "She lived in a burrow with. . ."

Baby Honeybun threw her blue bunny toy across the room.

"She lived in a burrow with a cuddly blue bunny and. . ."

Baby Honeybun threw her pink butterfly rattle across the room.

". . .and a noisy pink butterfly," said Pickles, who was beginning to get the hang of this. "One day," he went on, "something really terrible happened to Baby Honeybun. She was left all alone with two big monsters, called Penny and Pickles. And they were *horrible*!"

Baby Honeybun stopped yelling for a moment and made a kind of gurgling noise. It was almost as if she was laughing.

"Those horrible monsters did awful things," said Pickles. "They grabbed her and nearly dropped her. They made a terrible squeaky noise at her. And they woke her up when she was having a nice, quiet nap in the afternoon."

Baby Honeybun sighed again. For a whole two minutes she had forgotten to yell.

"The worst thing was," said Pickles, "that the monsters couldn't understand baby talk at all. This made Baby Honeybun so angry that all she could do was yell. Then she had a very good idea. She remembered that her cuddly blue bunny could speak lots of different languages, so she whispered in his ear what she wanted to say to the horrible monsters."

Pickles gently held the blue bunny close to Baby Honeybun. Then he held it up to his own furry ear.

"Is that so?" he asked, listening hard to the blue bunny. "Well, that is fine. Penny, please be quiet. Baby Honeybun wants to have a little nap."

And at that, Baby Honeybun gave a big yawn and closed her eyes.

When Mother Rabbit came back from her shopping a few minutes later, she found not one but *three* sleeping bunnies in her living room. And she was far too sensible to wake *any* of them.

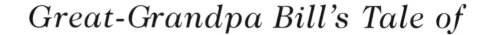

Great-Grandpa Bill's Tale of

How Things Used To Be

Great-Grandpa Bill cleared his throat. He was about to tell a story. As quietly as they could, several rabbits slipped out of the room and several others settled down for a little snooze. They had all heard Great-Grandpa's stories many, many times before, and it was very warm with so many bunnies sitting around the fire.

"When I was a young rabbit," said Great-Grandpa Bill, "things were very hard. We didn't have all the comforts that you young rabbits take for granted today. We didn't have any electricity or running water indoors. We had to go outside, even on the coldest days, and carry heavy buckets of water from the well. It wasn't an easy job, I can tell you, especially in the middle of winter when the well was frozen solid."

"What's a well?" asked a little voice from the back, only to be silenced by lots of "Shhhhhhhhs" from other bunnies. It took Great-Grandpa Bill long enough to tell his stories without little ones interrupting and making him lose his thread.

"We were very poor," Great-Grandpa Bill went on, causing another handful of bunnies to doze off, "and we had hardly any toys to play with. We had to make our own entertainment in those days. That's when I learned to juggle. Pass me those carrots, young Pickles."

Pickles passed the carrots, but several other bunnies slipped out of the room or down behind the sofa. The one thing that everyone knew about Great-Grandpa Bill's juggling was that he wasn't very good at it. True to form, in the next few minutes, he managed to break the glass in a picture frame and knock over a vase of flowers, soaking several bunnies in the process.

"And that's another thing," the old rabbit went on, chewing thoughtfully on one of his juggling carrots, "things in those days were made to last. They didn't tip over or fall apart like the flimsy things of today."

Two bunnies silently scuttled around clearing up the mess, as Great-Grandpa Bill droned on. More and more of his listeners were finding that his voice made them feel extraordinarily tired.

"Bunnies today have an easy life," said Grandpa. "Washing machines, vacuum cleaners, central heating . . . we didn't have any of those in the old days. But then, rabbits were made of sterner stuff then. Nowadays, most young rabbits couldn't do a hard day's work to save their lives. They've become soft."

Several bunnies who had so far only closed their eyes, now closed their ears as well. They had heard it all before.

Great-Grandpa Bill talked on for another half hour. He spoke of the difficulties of storing carrots in the days before refrigeration. He mused on the shortcomings of modern rabbits who no longer knew how to make their own soap. He remembered several rabbits in the past who had all expressed undying admiration for Great-Grandpa Bill.

At this point, the old rabbit called rather tetchily for a glass of water for his poor old throat. Years of pulling carrots in the frosty mornings of his youth had left him with a weakness in the vocal passages, he said. Poor Great-Grandma Lill shuffled off to bring him refreshments. She had heard his stories so many times before that she went onto automatic pilot as soon as Great-Grandpa Bill began clearing his throat.

"Ah, now, that's better," said the storyteller, taking a sip of water, "though it's not as good and cold as well-water used to be. Now, where was I?

Oh yes, I was just coming to the really exciting part of my story. It concerns the time I met a ferocious tiger in the woods."

Great-Grandpa Bill looked around expectantly. He expected a sharp intake of breath from his listeners as he gave this surprising news. But there was not a sound from anyone, except a very gentle snore from Great-Grandma Lill, who had held out longer than the rest of the sleeping audience.

Great-Grandpa Bill poked the fire in disgust. "It's just as I thought," he said. "Rabbits nowadays have no stamina. None at all."

Great-Grandma Guggles and
THE TALE THAT NEVER ENDS

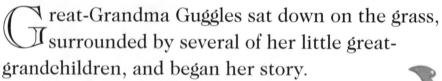

Great-Grandma Guggles sat down on the grass, surrounded by several of her little great-grandchildren, and began her story.

"Once upon a time," she said, "there was a young gentleman rabbit and a young lady rabbit who settled down together in a big family burrow in Warren Wood. Before long, they had five little baby bunnies. And goodness me, those babies were a trouble to their parents. They squiggled and wriggled all over the place."

"Like us?" asked the little bunnies, squiggling and wriggling themselves.

"Just like you," smiled Grandma Guggles. "But very, very slowly, the baby bunnies grew up. Soon they could ride their bicycles and write their own names all by themselves."

"We'll be able to do that soon," squeaked the little bunnies.

"Yes, indeed," agreed Great Grandma Guggles, "and pretty soon after that, you'll be almost grown-up and causing your parents all sorts of trouble all over again."

"What sort of trouble?" asked the little rabbits.

"Motorcycles," muttered the old lady darkly, "and short skirts and loud music. It's always the same with rabbits when they're nearly grown."

"Then what happens?" asked the little rabbits.

"Well, I don't know for sure what will happen to *you*," their great-grandmother went on, "but in this particular family, pretty soon those little rabbits were grown up and courting."

"Courting? What's courting?" asked one little rabbit curiously.

"I know," squeaked another. "It's lovey-dovey stuff and kissing and cuddling and not wanting little rabbits around."

"*Oooooh noooo!*" squealed the other bunnies. "We won't want to do that, not *ever*!"

"Well, I'm not so sure," said Great Grandma Guggles. "These rabbits I'm talking about, two by two they soon started wanting to settle down together in a big family burrow in Warren Wood. And before long, they had. . ."

"Baby bunnies! We know!" cried the little ones.

But Great Grandma Guggles shook her head. "These baby bunnies were special," she smiled. "These baby bunnies were *you*!"

THE
PUPPY
TALES
COLLECTION

Illustrated by
CATHIE SHUTTLEWORTH

Written by
NICOLA BAXTER

Mr. Bones the Baker Has

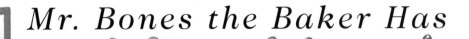

A Very Busy Day

There are times, as I'm sure you know, when your tummy suddenly feels as empty as a bowl without a bone. You need a snack, and you need it fast. If you should happen to find yourself in Houndsville, I recommend that you trot along, as fast as your paws will carry you, to Mr. Bones the Baker's shop. You won't need to ask any of the fine dogs of the town where to find it. Just point your nose into the air and sniff. Aaaaaahhh!

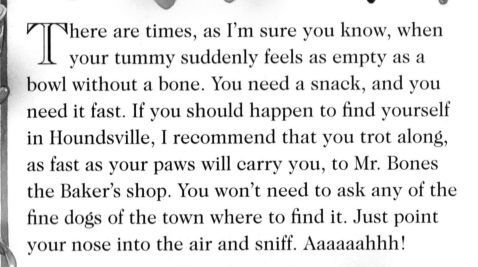

Like all bakers, Mr. Bones gets up before dawn to start making the pies and pastries for which he is famous. While the streetlamps still flicker yellow in the darkness, he is going about his business, mixing and measuring, cooking and cooling. Many of the dogs in Houndsville don't bother with alarm clocks. When the fourth batch of Mr. Bones' meat pies comes out of the oven, they *know* it is time for breakfast!

Mr. Bones has baked his way through days and weeks and years, but just recently he has begun to feel too old to be up before the sun. That is why a sign appeared in his shop this morning, advertising for an assistant.

Meanwhile, Mr. Bones must struggle on by himself. After the meat pies, which are easily his most popular item, he starts working on his cakes and pastries, which include such delights as bone-marrow rolls and fish dainties. No self-respecting dog in Houndsville would dream of sitting down to afternoon tea without some of these delicacies.

One morning, just as Mr. Bones was putting the finishing touches on his iced bone-jelly jubilees, he heard a rat-a-tat-tat at the shop door. He glanced at the clock. It was only half past six.

Mr. Bones felt a bit grumpy as he wiped his paws on his apron and hurried to the door. But his manner changed as soon as he saw who was there. It was Duchess Dulay, the most glamorous dog in Houndsville, even if she was now getting on in years. To tell you the truth, Mr. Bones had quite a soft spot for the Duchess, and he sometimes had rosy dreams of sharing his retirement with her.

But today Duchess Dulay's normally perfect grooming was a little windswept and wild. She looked upset, and Mr. Bones' tender heart immediately went out to her as he undid the bolts and flung open the door.

"My dear Duchess," he cried. "Whatever is the matter?"

"Oh, Mr. Bones," said the lady. She was close to tears. "I'm so sorry to disturb you at this time of the day, but I haven't been able to get a wink of sleep all night. Do you remember yesterday, when I was in your shop buying bone buns for my tea?"

"Yes, indeed," replied Mr. Bones. "You arrived just as I was checking my flour deliveries. I do apologize if I was not able to give you my full attention. Surely the bone buns didn't give you … that is, surely there was nothing wrong with the buns?" Mr. Bones wasn't sure it was polite to mention tummy upsets to a lady.

The Duchess quickly put his mind at rest. "No, no, my dear dog," she cried. "The buns were delicious as usual. It's my diamond bracelet!"

Mr. Bones waited. He didn't have the faintest idea what she was talking about.

"I lost it, you see," said the elegant dog. "Sometime during the day, yesterday, the clasp came loose and it slipped from my wrist. It's my own silly fault. I knew that the clasp was faulty and I should have asked Miss Ruby to fix it. How I wish I had!"

"But my dear lady," said Mr. Bones with an anxious frown, "what makes you think you lost it here?"

"By a process of elimination," said Duchess Dulay grandly.

Mr. Bones' visitor soon explained that she had retraced her steps of the day before, and at every place that she had stopped, someone or other could remember seeing the very glittery and eye-catching bracelet on her wrist.

"Yes! I remember seeing it myself," cried Mr. Bones. "It is very beautiful. Oh! But that means you were definitely wearing it when you arrived."

"Yes, and I certainly wasn't when I left," said the Duchess. "Never mind how I know that. I've figured it out. Now, let's do a thorough search for it. It can't have gone far,"

And much to Mr. Bones' distress, the grand lady got down on her paws and started searching vigorously under the shelves and the counter.

"Wait! Please wait!" cried Mr. Bones. "It simply can't be there! I sweep the shop very carefully every evening before I close up. I can assure you that I would have noticed a diamond bracelet. I pride myself on keeping the shop spotless."

Duchess Dulay straightened up, a little pink in the face. "Of course you do, Mr. Bones," she said. "I didn't mean to suggest otherwise. But where can the bracelet have gone?"

At just the same moment, the same awful thought came to both Mr. Bones and his visitor.

"The flour sacks!" she cried. "They were open so you could check them. The bracelet must have slipped inside!"

And without another word, she marched through the shop and straight to the back where the ovens were. "Where is the flour?" she cried. "Where do you store it?"

Mr. Bones waved his paw at the trays and trays of pies, cakes, and pastries that covered every surface. "I don't," he said simply. "I don't store it, I use it. All the flour that arrived yesterday has been made into the things you see before you. The bracelet must be *inside* one of these!"

There was an awful silence, as both dogs looked hopelessly around. Then Mr. Bones sprang into action.

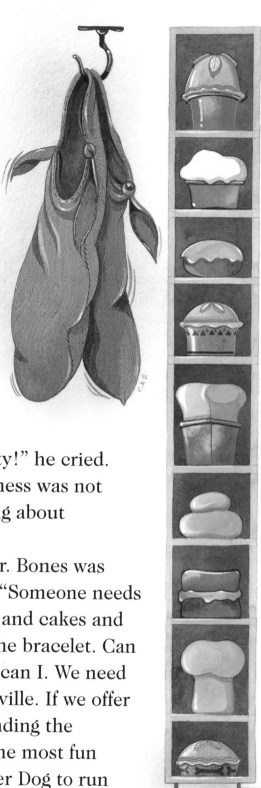

"What we need is a street party!" he cried. "Really, Mr. Bones!" The Duchess was not amused. "How can you be thinking about frivolities at a time like this?"

For the first time in his life, Mr. Bones was rather blunt with Duchess Dulay. "Someone needs to munch and chew all those pies and cakes and pastries," he said, "until we find the bracelet. Can you tackle so many? No? Neither can I. We need help from the fine dogs of Houndsville. If we offer free food and a little reward for finding the bracelet, everyone will think it's the most fun they've had in years. I'll ask Dasher Dog to run around and tell everyone."

Duchess Dulay looked at Mr. Bones with a new respect in her eyes. She had never heard him sound so masterful.

And the baker's idea turned out to be an excellent one. Almost all the dogs in Houndsville were happy to accept the invitation that Dasher Dog brought to them—after all, no dog in his right mind would ever turn down the chance to eat Mr. Bones' meat pies.

By lunchtime, several picnic tables in the street outside were groaning with goodies. And several dogs were groaning to get at them, especially in view of the very generous reward offered by Duchess Dulay.

"Just be careful with your teeth!" called Mr. Bones. "Remember that diamonds are very hard!"

🧁 And fifteen minutes later, Mr. Bones' idea was rewarded when a great shout went up at one table.

🧁 "I've found it!" cried a small poodle called Daphne. And everybody cheered.

🧁 Later that day, Duchess Dulay came to thank Mr. Bones for his help.

"Not at all, Duchess," replied the baker, looking flushed. "It was a pleasure."

🧁 "Please," said the Duchess, turning pink herself now, "do call me Davina."

"Only if you will call me Barker," said Mr. Bones firmly. "Allow me to escort you home, Davina."

🧁 And he offered her his arm.

Mrs. Gruff the Greengrocer Has

A Very Long Rest

Mrs. Gruff the Greengrocer had been feeling very tired recently, and she couldn't imagine why. It was true that she worked every day with her husband in their greengrocer's shop, and the shop was always very busy. In the evening, when she had locked the door behind the last customer, there was clearing up to be done and the day's earnings to be counted.

Of course, there was an early start every morning, too, when Mrs. Gruff went with her husband in their van to pick up fresh fruit and vegetables for the shop. But Mrs. Gruff had been doing all those things for years, and she had never felt the slightest bit tired. She loved chatting with the customers and finding out about *everything* that was going on in Houndsville.

"Perhaps I'm just getting old," she said to Mr. Gruff one evening, as she put her paws up at last.

"Nonsense, my dear," said that gentleman gallantly, putting on his comfy slippers. But … er … perhaps you're not quite as … er … sylphlike as once you were. Maybe that is making you tired."

Mr. Gruff knew he had made a mistake as soon as the words were out of his mouth.

"You mean I'm *fat*?" cried his wife, rushing to the mirror above the fireplace.

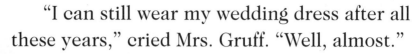

"I can still wear my wedding dress after all these years," cried Mrs. Gruff. "Well, almost."

Mr. Gruff succeeded in calming his wife down at last. He suggested it was time she took a rest from the business for a few days.

"I can ask Spotty Smith to help me out for a day or two," he said. "You just take it easy, my dear. And I will do all the cooking. At least, I'll buy us some delicious meals from Mr. Bones' shop. You won't have to do a thing."

Mrs. Gruff sighed. It was very tempting. She really did feel exhausted, and in fact, although she did not want to admit it to Mr. Gruff, she had found it difficult to button up her clothes recently. A few days of rest, eating healthy things and relaxing, would do her a world of good. It would be like going to a health farm while staying at home.

And Mrs. Gruff really did enjoy her rest. She lay on the sofa and read all the magazines she loved, such as *Hounds Beautiful* and *Pawsmopolitan*.

After a week, Mr. Gruff asked how she was feeling.

"Much better," said his wife. "But I still don't feel quite myself. Maybe a few more days' rest will do the trick."

So when customers inquired about his wife, Mr. Gruff simply said she was still resting.

One day, it was Dr. Fetch who asked. And when he heard the reply, he decided he should see how Mrs. Gruff was for himself.

"A young dog like you shouldn't be feeling tired all the time," he said when he saw her.

Mrs. Gruff sighed and yawned.
"But I still do, Doctor," she said. "And now it feels as if my dinner is jumping up and down in my tummy. Maybe there was something wrong with the meat pies we had for lunch today."

"If they were Mr. Bones' meat pies," said the doctor firmly, "there was nothing wrong with them at all, for I had them myself. Now then, let's see what the trouble is."

Dr. Fetch examined his patient and looked up in alarm.

"This is serious," he said. "We need to get you upstairs right away. And I think we should call your husband, too."

But Mr. Gruff was busy on the telephone, sorting out a pumpkin problem. It was over an hour later that he was given the message. At once, he left the shop in Spotty's paws and hurried home to see his wife.

Mr. Gruff was panting by the time he reached home. He found the front door open and ran anxiously up the stairs, three at a time. Whatever could be the matter? The doctor's message had sounded urgent.

As he burst into the bedroom, Mr. Gruff had the biggest surprise of his life, for there was his wife, sitting up in bed and looking as proud as a Pekinese. Tucked in beside her were five little puppies, fast asleep.

"But…" cried Mr. Gruff. "But… but… but… why didn't you tell me?"

"I didn't know," smiled his wife. "I was so busy working that I never thought about puppies. Are you pleased?"

"It's the most wonderful surprise I've ever had," gasped Mr. Gruff, giving her a hug. "But I suppose this means you'll be having an even longer rest now?"

"I've been thinking about that," said Mrs. Gruff sweetly. "And I don't think it's fair for me to do all the resting. We can take turns looking after the puppies … I mean resting … on alternate days."

Mr. Gruff agreed at once. But if you've ever had anything to do with young puppies, you'll know there was very little rest for any of the Gruff family for several years to come!

Sir Woofington Paws Has

A VERY WOBBLY CHIMNEY

Sir Woofington Paws lived in a large house a mile or so from the town of Houndsville. Unfortunately, although his family had once been very wealthy, Sir Woofington was now in reduced circumstances.

This was mostly his father's fault. Old Sir Patchmont Paws had been a great collector. Unfortunately, he hadn't had the vaguest idea what to collect. His famous art collection had turned out to be the work of a small team of professional forgers who could turn their paws to any style or period. Yes, even the famous picture of the Dog's Palace in Venice by Kenneletto was proved to be the work of Towser "The Paintbrush" Terrier, a dog well known to the Pooch Police.

It was the same with Sir Patchmont's collection of fine silver. He had bought it in good faith from a shifty-looking dog who knocked at the door one day. Only a week later, it was discovered that every single piece had been stolen from Duchess Dulay. Of course, it had to be returned.

I need hardly mention what happened to Sir Patchmont's ice-sculpture collection one hot June, or the most unfortunate scene when he discovered two of his nephews munching their way through his very expensive bone collection. It is enough to say that by the time he had finished, Sir Patchmont Paws had lost almost all the family money, leaving his son, Sir Woofington, to try to keep up appearances on a shoestring.

It had once been widely believed in Houndsville that Sir Woofington would marry the widowed Duchess Dulay, but he could not bring himself to propose to her when he had no way of supporting her. So Sir Woofington lived alone in his crumbling home, looking sadly at the spaces on the walls where his father's fake pictures had once hung.

Now Paws Place was literally falling down around Sir Woofington's ears. He couldn't afford to hire professionals to fix his roof or check his plumbing, so he did it himself. Sadly, Sir Woofington's home-improvement skills were dreadfully bad. He frequently made matters worse instead of better.

One morning, Sir Woofington was chopping wood outside the back door when he happened to look up. As he did so, a tiny bird landed on one of the tallest chimneys of the house, and … there could be no doubt about it … it quite distinctly wobbled. The chimney wobbled. The bird wobbled. And Sir Woofington, watching this with a sinking heart, felt his knees wobble too.

I'm afraid that Sir Woofington inherited his brains from his father. Before you could say, "Don't even think about it, Sir W.!" he hurried off to find the very longest ladder in his workshop.

Without waiting for someone to come and help him, Sir Woofington started to climb. Up, up, up he went. And wobble, wobble, wobble went the ladder. Every step brought him nearer to disaster—and every step was wobblier than the one before. But the silly dog kept climbing.

Just as Sir Woofington reached the base of the wobbly chimney, a car drove into his driveway. The climbing dog looked down. As he turned his head, the ladder slipped away, leaving him clinging to the chimney.

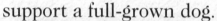

Sir Woofington Paws thought his last moments had come. In a faint voice, he called for help. Now that he was close to it, he could see that the chimney was likely to fall down in the slightest breeze. It certainly was not strong enough to support a full-grown dog.

Far below, a dog that Sir Woofington had never seen before looked up in horror at the dangling figure. He spotted a little window not far from Sir Woofington's left paw and, without waiting to knock or introduce himself, he rushed into the house and up the stairs. Just as Sir Woofington felt that he would have to let go, the strange dog grabbed him firmly with a large paw.

Half an hour later, Sir Woofington and his guest were drinking tea in the shabby dining room. (Sir Woofington couldn't afford real houndstooth tea, but his garden was full of nettles.) It was only then, after offering heartfelt thanks, that Sir Woofington asked his visitor why he had come.

To his host's surprise, the large dog flushed pink. "I have come," he said, "to put right a bad thing I did many years ago. When I was a young dog," he went on, "I turned to crime. One day I robbed the home of a rich dog in Houndsville and sold her silver to your father."

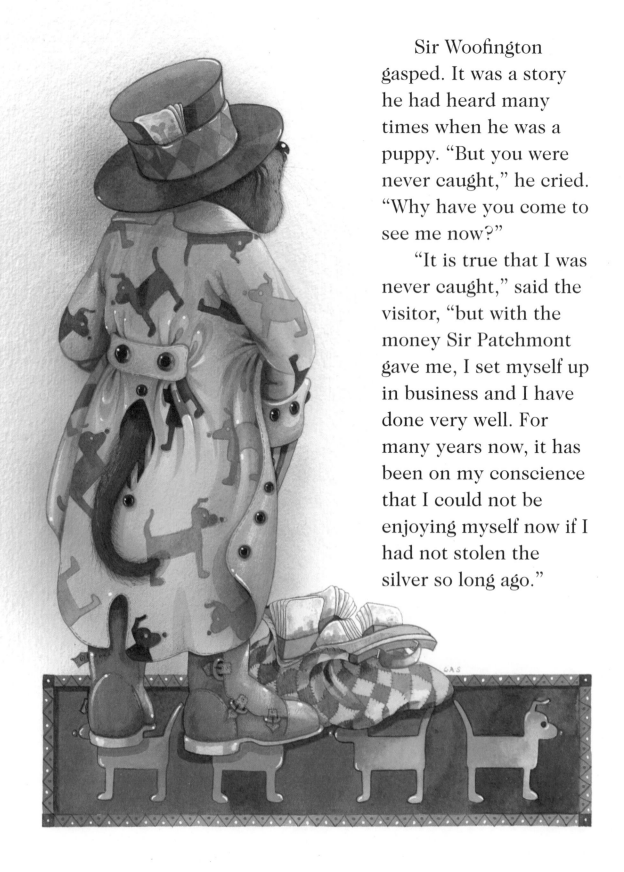

Sir Woofington gasped. It was a story he had heard many times when he was a puppy. "But you were never caught," he cried. "Why have you come to see me now?"

"It is true that I was never caught," said the visitor, "but with the money Sir Patchmont gave me, I set myself up in business and I have done very well. For many years now, it has been on my conscience that I could not be enjoying myself now if I had not stolen the silver so long ago."

"My dear sir," cried Sir Woofington, "this morning you saved my life. What is past is past. I am only too happy to forget the whole thing."

But the stranger shook his head. "You deserve to have half my wealth," he said. "There is plenty for both of us."

So that is how Sir Woofington's fortunes were restored. He is once more seen in the best circles in Houndsville. Paws Place has been repaired by skilled dogs and filled with fine furniture and some (absolutely genuine) pictures. And it is said that Duchess Dulay has been seen dining there recently on more than one occasion!

Mr. Woof the Watchmaker Has

A Very Merry Christmas

When all the dogs of Houndsville are sleeping peacefully in their beds (except Mr. Gruff, who is probably feeding one of his troublesome little puppies), Mr. Woof the Watchmaker is often lying awake, with every hair quivering and his ears twitching eagerly. Is he afraid of things that go bump in the night? No, Mr. Woof is anxious about things that go clang in the night. Or rather, of things that go *clang, dong, ding, bong, ping* in the night!

The poor dog lies there waiting for the clocks in the town to chime. He is dreadfully, dreadfully afraid that one of them will be silent. If it is—and, after all, any clock might go wrong at some time—he fears other dogs will say, "You know, old Woof isn't up to the job any more. He should retire. The church clock has gone wrong three times this year." Mr. Woof doesn't want to retire. He worries about what life might be like without watches to repair and clocks to care for.

Five clocks chime every hour of the day and night in Houndsville—the church clock, the school clock, the Town Hall clock, the station clock, and the clock above Mr. Woof's shop. They all make different sounds, but the old watchmaker recognizes them all. At one o'clock in the morning, he hears them chiming once. *Clang! Dong! Ding! Bong! Ping!* At two o'clock he hears them chime twice. *Clang! Clang! Dong! Dong! Ding! Ding! Bong! Bong! Ping! Ping!* And on it goes.

Even when Mr. Woof finally falls asleep, his ears are awake, waiting for something to go wrong.

At Christmas, Mr. Woof is even more worried than usual. If the clocks go wrong, how will the dogs who sing carols in the town square know when to begin? How will puppies know when to open their presents? In fact, how will any dog know that Christmas has arrived at last?

Now, Mr. Woof's fears about growing older are not completely silly. He is not as lively a dog as he once was. His paws are not as nimble, and his eyesight is not as sharp. He is also only too aware that his young nephew, Hunter Houndly, is building up a flourishing business on the other side of town. Mr. Woof taught Hunter everything he knows. He planned that Hunter would take over his business, but when the time came, he found that he just couldn't stop.

Not unreasonably, Hunter pointed out that now that he was trained, he wanted to be a real watchmaker. He had no choice but to open his own shop. Mr. Woof was proud of him, but he was anxious too.

In fact, Mr. Woof was so worried that he had become quite unable to think sensibly about the situation. And the more nights he spent lying awake, the less sensible he was able to be. He was making himself ill, and everyone could see it, but no one could think of a way to bring him to his senses.

At last, though, a snowstorm came to the rescue.
It was the worst snowstorm ever to hit Houndsville,
and it happened on Christmas Eve. The first flakes
began fluttering down in the morning. By the
afternoon, it was snowing heavily. By the time
darkness fell, traffic could no longer travel on the
snow-filled streets of Houndsville. Dogs hurrying
home, bundled up against the cold, told each other
how lucky it was that the snow had come on
Christmas Eve, when everyone wanted to be at home
with their families anyway. And, of course, all the
little puppies squealed with delight to see their town
looking just like an old-fashioned Christmas card.

Mr. Woof heard all the clocks of the town strike six, but the sound was muffled by the snow. He was so tired after he had sold the final last-minute present and closed up his shop that he decided to go straight to bed. He fell asleep at once.

Which is why, some time later, Mr. Woof didn't hear the five clocks striking seven … or eight … or nine. At least, it wasn't because he was asleep that he didn't hear them, but because they didn't strike. Snow had muffled their chimes and clogged up their mechanisms. Every one of them was silent. Mr. Woof slept on.

Christmas Day dawned bright ... and white. Outside, the whole town sparkled in the sunshine. Mr. Woof awoke and knew at once that something wonderful had happened. He had enjoyed a whole night's sleep! He felt young and refreshed! He felt full of the joys of Christmas! And, more than anything else, he felt, now that he could think clearly, that he had been a very silly dog. Mr. Woof didn't waste any time. He quickly wrapped up a very special present and set off for Hunter Houndly's house.

As he padded through the snow, he couldn't help noticing that the silent clocks had not stopped any of the fun in Houndsville. The singers were howling their heads off in the town square. Puppies everywhere were squealing over their new presents. Everyone looked cheerful. "Merry Christmas, Mr. Woof!" they called, as he walked by. Not one of them mentioned the clocks.

Mr. Woof smiled to himself as he reached Hunter Houndly's door and rang the bell. "Season's Greetings, Hunter!" he cried, as his nephew opened the door. "Here's a present for you."

Hunter gasped as he tore off the paper. "It's the key to my shop," confirmed his uncle, "or rather, it's the key to *your* shop. I'm not going to worry about clocks now. Oh, and by the way, I think you should take a look at the clock above the shop. It seems to have stopped. Not a very good advertisement for a watchmaker, is it? Merry Christmas!"

Mrs. Trot the Toy Seller Has A VERY BIG PROBLEM

One afternoon, Mrs. Trot was just about to close her toyshop for the day when Mrs. Muncher knocked urgently on the door.

"Oh! I am so glad you haven't closed!" she cried. "I have to buy a present for one of the little Gruff puppies. Young George Gruff is my godson, you know, and I promised him a special present if he stopped chewing his daddy's ears. I hear he's been as good as gold this week, so I must keep my promise."

"Of course," agreed Mrs. Trot. "What kind of present did you have in mind?"

"Oh, something small," replied her customer. "In fact, I know just what he would like—a toy elephant. He's got a little book about one, and he really loves it."

Mrs. Trot looked around her shelves. There were toy pandas and giraffes and tigers. There were cuddly polar bears and fluffy zebras. But there were no elephants at all.

"Don't worry!" cried Mrs. Trot. "I can telephone the warehouse in Dogborough and ask them to make an overnight delivery. They supply anything you could ever want. Lots of the shops in town use them. Just leave it to me. If you stop by tomorrow morning, on your way to see young George, I'll have the elephant ready and waiting. I'll even wrap it for you if you like."

"That would be perfect," smiled Mrs. Muncher.

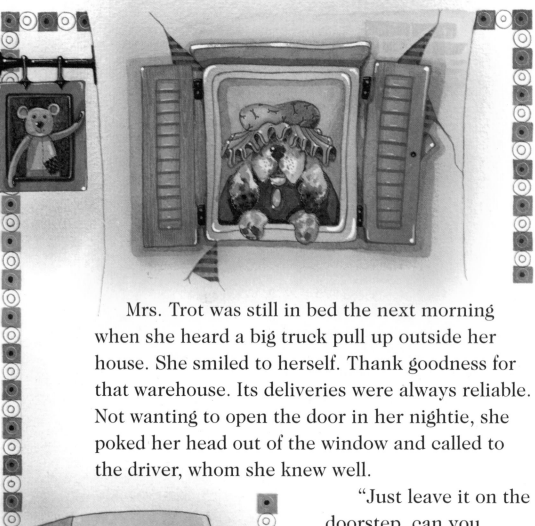

Mrs. Trot was still in bed the next morning when she heard a big truck pull up outside her house. She smiled to herself. Thank goodness for that warehouse. Its deliveries were always reliable. Not wanting to open the door in her nightie, she poked her head out of the window and called to the driver, whom she knew well.

"Just leave it on the doorstep, can you, Dasher? I'll be down in a minute, but I don't want to hold you up."

"No problem!" called the delivery dog. "Shall I tie it to the door knocker, so it doesn't wander off? I've got some strong string in the truck."

But Mrs. Trot's head had disappeared from the window. She was busily getting dressed so she could wrap the toy before Mrs. Muncher arrived.

Dasher shook his head and went to open the doors of the truck.

In fact, Mrs. Trot was not able to get ready as quickly as she had hoped. Just as she was buttoning her skirt, the telephone by her bed rang. It was her cousin, who lived in China!

Of course, Mrs. Trot couldn't just put the phone down. She chatted for a long time, forgetting the package on the doorstep. When she finished at last, she looked at her watch in dismay. Mrs. Muncher was due any minute!

Scuttling down the stairs, Mrs. Trot reached the front door in three seconds flat. She flung open the door and found…

a real elephant!

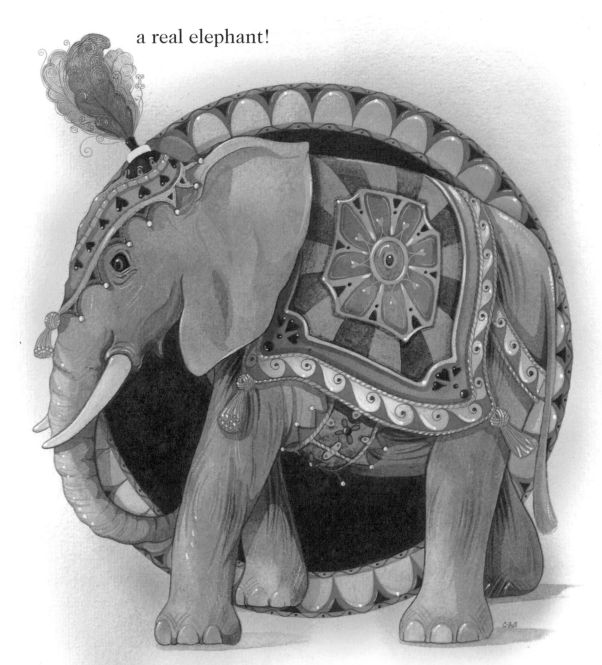

Just at that moment, Mrs. Muncher arrived.
"I said a *small* present!" she gasped.
"I'm afraid I haven't had time to wrap it," cried
Mrs. Trot.
Then they both started laughing so hard the
tears ran down their whiskers.

Luckily, it didn't take long for the mix-up to be sorted out. Dasher returned with a much smaller elephant and took charge of the larger one.

"I'm sorry," he said. "This fellow was on his way home to India, but the labels must have got mixed up. It's not often we have two elephant deliveries on one day."

Just then, the elephant stuck his trunk into the rain barrel outside Mrs. Trot's shop and did what elephants do. Mrs. Trot and Mrs. Muncher jumped out of the way just in time.

"Never mind!" laughed Mrs. Trot. "My shop window did need washing! It's been a most interesting day so far!"

"And I've got a wonderful story to tell my godson," smiled Mrs. Muncher. "It's much better than the one in his storybook!"

Dasher the Delivery Dog Has
A Very Strange Package

Dasher the Delivery Dog often laughed about the jobs he had to do. It was lucky that he was such a lively, cheerful dog, because his customers were sometimes very difficult. One elderly dog changed her mind three times about where she wanted her new piano—and then sent it back to the shop after all.

In his working life, Dasher had been asked to deliver many strange things, and he always did it with his usual friendly smile, until one day he had a package for the Perfect Poodle Beauty Salon.

The Salon was run by Miss Evangeline Puff, a dog who would never dream of appearing in public without at least seven bows in her hair and probably some frills and ribbons as well.

Before he made a delivery to her shop, Dasher always tried to guess whether today her hair would be pink, or yellow, or blue, or green, or the vivid shade of purple Evangeline chose when she needed cheering up.

On this particular morning, Dasher picked up his packages from the depot as usual and decided to deliver the one for the Perfect Poodle Beauty Salon first, since it was the nearest. He put the package beside him on the seat of his delivery truck and set off. As he did so, Dasher couldn't help noticing that the package had been sent from Brazil, and he gave a little shudder.

What, you may ask, was so terrible about Brazil? It's a wonderful country. But Dasher knew that Brazil had miles and miles of rich, lush, tropical forest. And where there is rich, lush, tropical forest, there are creepy things, and crawly things, and little skittery, nibbling creatures. And where there are *those*, there are sometimes great big red hairy spiders. Dasher wasn't afraid of *anything*—except great big red hairy spiders. The very thought of one of those made him shivery all over.

Dasher knew that Evangeline was not likely to have started ordering spiders for her Salon, but he kept a careful eye on the package all the same.

All went well, until Dasher whizzed around a corner and found a group of little puppies about to cross the road with their teacher Mr. Terrier. Dasher slammed on his brakes and stopped safely, but as he did so, the package from Brazil flew off the seat and onto the floor. Dasher waved to Mr. Terrier and the puppies, then stooped to pick up the package. The fall had torn the paper a little, and the string was getting looser and looser by the second. To Dasher's horror, he distinctly saw some red hairy stuff poking out of the torn paper—and it was moving!

As a matter of fact, the package was moving because Dasher's paws were trembling, but he didn't think of that. He slammed the truck into gear and set off the second the puppies were safely across the road.

Poor Dasher really was flustered with fear. He didn't know what to do except drive as quickly as he safely could to Evangeline Puff's Salon. But all the time he was driving, he imagined the biggest, reddest, hairiest spider in the world slowly creeping out of the package beside him. The thought was so very horrible that he didn't even dare to look at the package. He drove with his eyes straight ahead and his paws gripping the wheel as if his life depended on it.

As Mr. Bones told
Duchess Dulay when
they had lunch together
later that day, "Old
Dasher really was
dashing this morning.
And he was in such a
hurry, he didn't even
wave to me."

Waving was the last thing on Dasher's mind.
Any second, he expected to feel a soft touch on his
knee as the spider began to climb across to his
side of the truck.

When Dasher pulled up outside the Perfect
Poodle Beauty Salon, his nerves were at breaking
point. He forgot to guess whether Evangeline
would be blue or pink. He just rushed inside and
flung himself down in a chair.

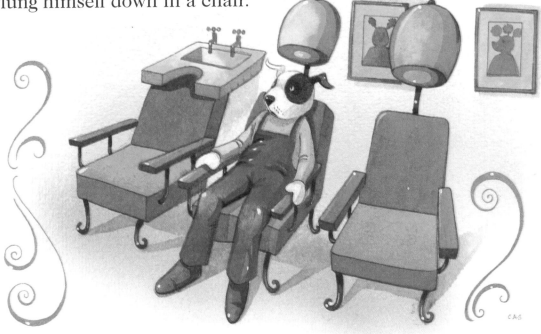

"There's a package for you in my truck," he gasped. "Can you get it, please? I'll just wait right over here and hurry off when you've got it." And he scuttled over to the farthest corner of the Salon.

Evangeline Puff was surprised, but she did what Dasher asked. She read a lot of novels in her spare time, with glamorous heroines and daring heroes. It flashed across her mind that maybe Dasher was being chased by a gang of enemy spies. How exciting!

But outside, she found her package easily and, except for the corner being a little torn, it looked fine.

"I'm so glad this has arrived, Dasher," said Evangline, coming back into her Salon. "Look!"

Dasher almost fainted as Evangline tore open the package to reveal … an amazing red wig with sequins and tropical flowers all over it!

When Dasher had recovered from the shock, he
was so relieved he told Evangeline the whole story.

"Poor Dasher," she cried. "Let me give you a
special haircut to make you feel better."

But Dasher, looking at the very elaborate
hairstyles shown around the walls, said no politely
and went on his way. Although there's nothing
quite as frightening as a great big red hairy spider
from Brazil, let's face it, Evangeline's hairstyles
come pretty close!

Mr. Terrier the Teacher Has
A VERY ODD FEELING

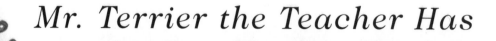

Puppies, as I'm sure you know, can be naughtier than almost any other little animals. They chew things. They sharpen their little claws on things. And when they are very small, I'm afraid they sometimes leave little … er … *puddles* around the place. You can imagine that teaching a whole class of puppies is not an easy job. Mr. Terrier the Teacher felt that he needed five pairs of paws and eyes in the back of his head.

One morning, when Mr. Terrier took off his hat and began to write on the board about the important subject of lampposts and how to use them, he heard a lot of giggling going on at the back of the room.

"Ruffles! Rupert! Randall! Is that you?" he called, knowing that the naughty triplets were often at the bottom of any trouble.

But the three little dogs spoke up at once with solemn faces.

"No, sir!"

"No, sir!"

"No, sir!"

Mr. Terrier frowned and turned back to his writing. But now the giggling was louder than ever. Mr. Terrier spun around as quickly as he could, his ears flying. In fact, he turned so quickly he felt dizzy and had to clutch at his desk.

He was not quick enough. As the room revolved gently around him, all the poor teacher could see was twenty innocent little faces looking up at him. Slowly, he turned back to his work.

This time, the giggling was uncontrolled. When Mr. Terrier turned around, he saw little puppies rolling on the floor with merriment. Some even had tears of laughter dripping from their whiskers.

Mr. Terrier used his iciest tones.

"Would someone please tell me just *what* is so funny? Well? *Ooooooh!*"

Just at that moment, Mr. Terrier felt a very odd feeling where his shirt collar met his neck. It was slithery and slimy and squirmy and enough to make even the bravest dog run yelping to his mother. Mr. Terrier would have done just that if it were not for the fact that twenty pairs of naughty eyes were watching him eagerly. And twenty pink tongues were panting with glee.

"Rupert!" called the teacher. "Would you come here a minute, please?" It took all Mr. Terrier's self-control not to start squealing.

Rupert trotted to the front of the class, looking a little apprehensive.

"I wonder," said Mr. Terrier, "if you would mind removing the snake that is wriggling down my neck. I wouldn't want it to get squashed."

Mr. Terrier was determined to remain cool and calm. It would take more than a slithering reptile to frighten *him*.

Rupert looked puzzled.

"There isn't a snake wriggling down your neck, sir," he said. "No snake at all."

"Well, the lizard then," said Mr. Terrier, feeling more uncomfortable by the second, but determined not to show it. "Don't split hairs with me, young puppy."

"There's no lizard either, sir," said Rupert, looking horribly truthful.

"Is it a spider? Is it a worm? Is it a centipede?" asked Mr. Terrier, his voice rising with every question. Then he had an even worse thought. "Is it," he squeaked, "a frog?"

"Sir, are you feeling well?" asked Rupert, looking concerned. "Why don't you sit down? It is hot in here."

Mr. Terrier could feel the slithering and sliding getting worse and worse. He simply couldn't bear it any more. Visions of tarantulas, toads, and things that crawl out from under rocks filled his head. He gave a little cry and pulled off his coat, flinging it on the floor.

From out of the coat, something red and yellow and slimy began to crawl. Mr. Terrier stepped back in horror. Was it some alien life form, ready to take over the world?

But as he looked, horrified, at the horrible stuff, Mr. Terrier's nose began to twitch. When a dog's eyes are playing tricks on him, his nose will often set him straight. And this time, Mr. Terrier's nose was telling him something very strange. It was telling him that the slimy yellow and red crawling stuff was … plums and custard!

Mr. Terrier took a step forward. He looked carefully at the mess on the floor. It smelled like plums and custard. It looked like plums and custard. Mr. Terrier stooped down and put out a cautious paw. He raised the paw to his mouth. There was no doubt about it, it *was* plums and custard! Lots of it!

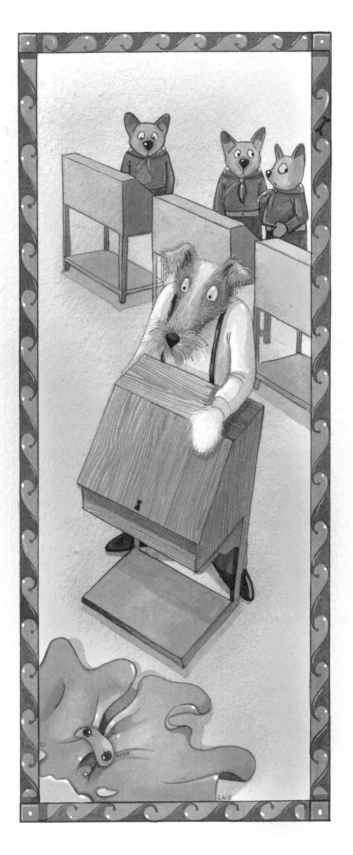

Mr. Terrier was angry. He was very angry indeed. Wiping the back of his neck with his handkerchief as best he could, he faced the class.

"Which of you naughty, nasty, *silly* little puppies has done this?" he asked. "And," he went on, as a thought struck him, "how?"

Mr. Terrier looked at the ceiling for a hanging bucket of dripping custard. There wasn't one.

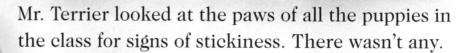

Mr. Terrier looked at the paws of all the puppies in the class for signs of stickiness. There wasn't any.

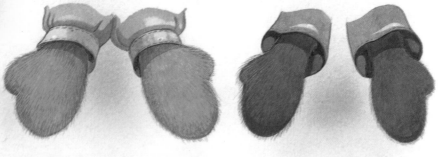

Mr. Terrier looked under desks and inside schoolbags for spoons or bowls or cartons. There weren't any.

And then, at the back of Mr. Terrier's mind, there came a little whispering thought. It told him his elderly mother had been making supper last night. It told him she had been called to the telephone just as she was pouring something into a big bowl. It told him that, as he handed her the telephone, he had also put his hat down on the table. It also told him he had rushed to work this morning without stopping to think about anything, even the slightly strange way his hat felt as it sat on his head.

"Puppies!" said Mr. Terrier. "I owe you an apology. I know now that you did not put snakes, or lizards, or worms, or frogs, or tarantulas, or plums and custard on my head or down my back. The culprit … and I will not hesitate to name him … was … ME! Sometimes old dogs can be as silly as young ones. Now I must go and clean myself up."

And it is an even stranger thing that all those puppies liked Mr. Terrier a lot more after that, and they were never as naughty again.

Old Mrs. Merrypaws Has A Very Welcome Visitor

Houndsville is a wonderful place to live. The summers are hot and sunny. The winters are cold and snowy. But just sometimes, in that in-between time that is not quite winter and not quite spring, there is rain … and more rain … and even more rain for day after day after day.

Mrs. Merrypaws looked out of her window one day and saw dark clouds above the trees beside the road. She shook her head anxiously.

"Only once in my life have I seen clouds like that," she told Mr. Clipped next door. "That was before the Great Flood."

Mr. Clipped shuddered. The Great Flood was before his time, but he had heard older dogs talking about it. He decided there and then to visit his sister a hundred miles away.

Mrs. Merrypaws decided she must be prepared for the worst. She began to make lists of the things she would need: food—lots of it—in cans and jars and waterproof packages; warm, waterproof clothes; sandbags to stop the water from coming in under the front door; a small inflatable boat if the worst came to the worst. For Mrs. Merrypaws felt that she was too old to swim to safety these days.

No sooner had Mrs. Merrypaws made her arrangements than it started to rain.

"Just as I thought," she said, looking out at the puddles on her path. "It won't be long now."

That night, Mrs. Merrypaws was well prepared when she went to bed. She had all her provisions and emergency equipment piled around her bed. In fact, it was piled so high, she couldn't see out of the window.

"I'm going to take a long, hot bath before bed," said the old dog to herself. "It may be the last one I can have for some time."

Later, tucked in her bed, Mrs. Merrypaws heard the howling of the wind and the lashing of the rain on the window as she closed her eyes.

Next morning, Mrs. Merrypaws woke to the sound of the swish-swash of water. She put one paw out of bed as usual and felt for her slipper. Instead, her toes touched something cold and wet. Peering over the edge of her bed, she saw to her horror that there was water all around!

"If there is water up here, the whole ground floor of the house must be flooded already!" said Mrs. Merrypaws. "Thank goodness I brought everything up here last night!"

Just then, a cheery voice called from the window. "Granny! Are you all right?"

It was Gerry, Mrs. Merrypaws' grandson. "Wait a moment!" called Mrs. Merrypaws, wading across the floor. But when she reached the window at last, she found to her astonishment that Gerry was not in a boat but up a ladder!

"You didn't hear me downstairs," he explained, "so I thought I'd check that you were all right."

Mrs. Merrypaws stared in disbelief at the scene outside the window. The sun was shining. There was not a puddle on the path. Then she looked at the scene inside. The sound of rushing water could still be heard, but now, suddenly, it sounded suspiciously like an overflowing bathtub.

"I'll be down in a minute," she told Gerry. "But in the meantime, let me give you some advice. If you worry too much about what *might* happen, you might not notice what *is* happening in front of your nose."

Young Gerry never did really understand what she was talking about, but I think we do, don't we?

Mr. Wag the Window Cleaner Has
A Very Shaky Start

No wonder the windows in Houndsville are so bright and shining. Every day, Mr. Wag the Window Cleaner is up on his ladder, working hard.

Now window cleaners, as I'm sure you know, see all kinds of things as they go about their business. It's hard not to notice what is happening on the other side of a sheet of glass—especially when it is extra clean! But Mr. Wag had a very strict rule: he never, ever gossiped about what he saw. He just tried to forget he had ever seen it.

It was on a sunny morning in early summer that Mr. Wag's rule was tested to its limits. He'd just arrived to clean Duchess Dulay's windows when he met Mr. Bones on the doorstep.

Mr. Bones, usually a most polite and courteous dog, barely said hello. He was nervously squashing his hat between his paws and clutching a large bouquet of flowers under his arm.

Mr. Wag smiled knowingly. It was well known that Duchess Dulay had recently hired a very pretty cook. No doubt Mr. Bones had come to call on her.

Mr. Wag climbed his ladder and began work on the living room windows. He was too busy to notice what was going on inside, and had just begun to slosh on the water, when he suddenly heard a scream.

"Oooooerrrrr!" Mr. Wag grabbed desperately at the window as his ladder wobbled alarmingly. Then, still somewhat shaken, Mr. Wag peered through the glass.

Inside, he saw Duchess Dulay … and Mr. Bones. And … oh, my goodness! … Mr. Bones seemed to be strangling her!

Mr. Wag didn't hesitate. He dropped his bucket to the ground far below and flung open the window. Then he hurled himself into the room.

"What's going on here?" he cried loudly, as he landed with a thump on the living room carpet.

"I beg your pardon!" gasped Duchess Dulay in horror. "What is the meaning of this?"

It was only then that Mr. Wag suddenly realized that Mr. Bones hadn't been strangling Duchess Dulay at all. He had been kissing her! And what was more, Duchess Dulay had been kissing him right back!

Mr. Wag wished the floor would open up and swallow him. He had broken a window. He had made a complete fool of himself. And he had probably lost two of his very best customers. Mumbling miserably, he tried to explain.

But the Duchess was smiling, and Mr. Bones stepped forward.

"This has been a very eventful morning," he said. "Mr. Wag, I would like to be the first to introduce you to the future Mrs. Bones."

"Oh, Barker," sighed the Duchess, "you always know *exactly* the right thing to say!"

A Very Famous Customer

Miss Bark loved working in her bookshop. It wasn't because she had lots of customers and made a good living. In fact, she had very few customers and had been known to give books away to dogs she thought would like them. No, what Miss Bark loved about her shop was that it gave her the chance to *read* all day. From morning until night, she sat in her comfy armchair and read all the books she liked best—and that was usually detective stories, the more complicated the better.

The books Miss Bark loved best of all were the Bloodhound Bungay stories by D. O. Gnaw. In these a bloodhound (of course), called Bungay (of course), *always* caught the criminal (of course)!

One morning, Miss Bark had just reached the
most exciting part of a Bloodhound Bungay
mystery called *The Hidden Pawprint*, when the
shop doorbell rang.

"Bother!" said Miss Bark, under her breath.
But she hurried forward anyway.

"Can I help you, sir?" she asked the tall,
distinguished-looking dog who had just entered.

You can imagine how surprised she was when
the visitor replied, "Yes. Do you have any of the
works of D. O. Gnaw? I am referring to the
Bloodhound Bungay stories, of course."

"I have all of them!" cried Miss Bark. "Every
one from *The Mysterious Matter of the Tail that
Wagged* to *Bungay's Final Case.*"

"Ah," said the customer, "that is excellent, but it is one book in particular I am looking for. I used to have a copy, but I lost it. I know it is not being printed any longer and very hard to find. It is called *The Hidden Pawprint*. I am willing to pay a large sum of money for it."

Poor Miss Bark was terribly torn. On the one paw, she badly needed some money to repair the heating system before winter arrived. On the other paw, she had only one precious copy of that book herself—and she hadn't finished reading it!

Miss Bark felt desperate. She simply couldn't make up her mind what to do. At last, she found herself telling her customer about her problem!

The customer smiled. "If you have reached the exciting part, you must be near the end," he said. "What if I sat down here and waited for you to finish? Then you could sell me the book."

So Miss Bark supplied him with a cup of coffee and a comfy chair and went back to reading her book. Almost an hour later, she closed it with a snap and a satisfied sigh.

"It was excellent," she said. "And I didn't guess the criminal until two pages before the end."

"Praise indeed," smiled the customer, as he put the book into his pocket and handed over a really very large sum of money.

Miss Bark thought that was the end of the matter. Then, almost a year later, a package arrived for her. Inside was a copy of a brand new edition of *The Hidden Pawprint!*

Miss Bark stared in disbelief at the first page of the book. It said:

DEDICATED TO MISS BARK,
MY MOST DEVOTED READER

As Miss Bark's paws trembled, a small piece of paper fluttered to the ground. She has kept it to this day:

My publisher needed a copy to print this new edition, and you were kind enough to find me one. I hope you enjoy it just as much the second time around.
With grateful thanks,
D. O. Gnaw

A Very Scary Night

Miss Dig sighed with pleasure. A rippling stream of silver and gold satin ran across her workroom, gleaming in the sunlight. The dressmaker's paws trembled as she began to cut it.

The satin was for Duchess Dulay's wedding dress, and the wedding was only days away. Miss Dig worked on, late into the night.

Miss Dig was young and enthusiastic, but she had been up since dawn. As the summer moon rose in the sky, her head drooped and she fell asleep right there in the workroom, surrounded by a sea of silver and gold.

It was midnight when the church clock's clanging caused Miss Dig to stir. As she opened her sleepy eyes, she saw a horrifying sight. Coming toward her, billowing in the breeze from the open window, was a gruesome shape. It seemed to glow and shimmer as it moved, looking like no dog she had ever seen.

Miss Dig was too
frightened even to
howl. The eerie
chiming of the clock
seemed to fill her head.
And still the shining
figure came forward.
With a little gasp, Miss
Dig grasped a vase of
flowers from the table
and flung it at the
shape ... which
collapsed on the floor.

It was only then Miss Dig saw that it was just
some of the Duchess's satin, blown by the breeze.
But what had she done? Across the fabric was a
huge stain, where water from the vase had soaked
into it. There was nothing the poor dog could do—
except wait for the water to dry and see if the
stain showed.

Miss Dig went to bed. She didn't expect to
sleep, but she did. In the morning, she came down
to the workroom, clasping her paws together to
stop them from shaking.

There lay the silver and gold satin, shining in
the sunlight once more. It looked perfect. Miss
Dig sighed and smiled. Of the two frights of
the past few hours, the second had been
much worse than the first. It certainly
had been a very scary night.

Mrs. Marrow the Caterer Has

A Very Special Job

Catering for a wedding at which two hundred of the top dogs in the area will be present is hard enough, but when the bridegroom is himself a famous and well-loved baker, the job becomes very difficult indeed.

Poor Mrs. Marrow was used to supplying food for big occasions. She was not used to having Mr. Bones peering over her shoulder every five minutes. He was a kind dog, but he was, naturally, nervous about his wedding. He so wanted everything to be perfect.

"Oh, Mrs. Marrow," he would say, "are you sure a bone soufflé is a good idea? The young puppies will make such a mess on the carpets. All the Gruff little ones are bridesmaids and pages, you know."

"It will be wonderful," said Mrs. Marrow firmly.

"And will the cake be finished in time?"

"It will be wonderful," said the caterer.

"Do you think the food will still look attractive with all those flowers around it?"

"It will be wonderful," smiled Mrs. Marrow.

As you can tell by now, Mrs. Marrow had one reply for all questions. It made Mr. Bones worry even more. Did she really know what she was doing? He decided to set a little trap.

"Mrs. Marrow," he cried, "I've decided after all to use black tablecloths and plastic spoons. Do you think that will be all right?"

"It will be wonderful," said Mrs. Marrow.

Now Mr. Bones was dreadfully worried. In fact, he was so concerned about the catering, he almost forgot to get ready for the wedding, and Dasher the Delivery Dog had to dash as he had never dashed before to get him to the church on time.

But the moment Mr. Bones saw Duchess Dulay in her beautiful dress, all his worries disappeared.

"Do you promise to love her and help her to the end of your days?" asked the priest, and Mr. Bones forgot himself entirely.

"It will be wonderful," he sighed.

It certainly was the most beautiful wedding ever seen in Houndsville—and there's no need to worry, the food was wonderful, too!